HAIRLESS HARASSMENT

Pet Whisperer P.I.

MOLLY FITZ

Editor: Megan Harris
Proofreader: Tabitha Kocsis
Cover Designer: Lou Harper, Cover Affairs

SWEET PROMISE PRESS
PO BOX 72
BRIGHTON, MI 48116

AUTHOR'S NOTE

Hey, new reader friend!

Welcome to the crazy inner workings of my brain. I hope you'll find it a fun and exciting place to be.

If you love animals as much as I do, then I'm pretty sure you're going to enjoy the journey ahead.

Hairless Harassment is one of my first brain-tickling adventures! Many more will be coming soon, so make sure you sign up for my newsletter or download my app to help you stay in the know. Doing so also unlocks adorable pictures of my own personal feline overlord, Schrödinger, deleted scenes from my books, bonus giveaways, and other cool things that are just for my inner circle of readers.

You can download my free app here:
mollymysteries.com/app

Or sign up for my newsletter here:
mollymysteries.com/subscribe

Okay, ready to talk to some animals and solve some mysteries?

Let's do this!
Molly Fitz

To anyone who wishes she could talk to her animal best friend… Well, what's stopping you?

CHAPTER ONE

Hi, I'm Angie Russo, and my pet cat never ever stops talking. Not just mews and meows, but actual words that I can understand. So far, I'm the only one who seems to have this ability, and I still have absolutely no idea why.

It all started when I got zapped by a faulty coffee maker at the law firm where I work as a paralegal. Since then, Octo-Cat and I have used our special connection to solve two murder investigations together. Yeah, even I have to admit, we make a pretty great team.

Only a few weeks have passed since our super sleuthing earned the local handyman Brock Calhoun a *get-out-of-jail-free* card. And already my feline sidekick is begging for another case. Apparently, napping and complaining all day isn't an exciting enough life for him now.

All my life I've been on the search for that one amazing talent that would make me special and give me purpose. My nan starred on Broadway in her prime, and my parents both work for the local news station and love what they do.

They were all so sure of their talents early in life, but I've really struggled to pinpoint mine. I couldn't even figure out my passion well enough to nail down a bachelor's degree, racking up seven associate degrees instead.

I definitely never expected to find my true calling as a paralegal, especially considering how much I've always hated lawyers. But now that I have Octo-Cat and my special ability, I find that working at the offices of Thompson, Longfellow & Associates provides the perfect way to use my new-found abilities for good—especially considering that the newest partner knows all about my ability to speak to animals.

Oh, yeah! Charles didn't get fired. Instead, he got promoted. I was so proud of him that I even suggested we go back to the Little Dog Diner in

Misty Harbor to celebrate with the world's best lobster rolls. He told me it would have to be some other time, though, because he already had plans with his new girlfriend, Breanne Calhoun.

Yeah, I don't get that, either.

The news that he'd started dating the cold and snippy realtor we'd very recently suspected of murder was enough to extinguish my crush on Charles once and for all, though. I've also decided that the next time Octo-Cat refers to him as "Upchuck," I'm not going to correct him.

The thought of him and Breanne together makes me sick, too.

It's for the best, though, I suppose. I really need to focus on understanding my new pet-whispering abilities, and Octo-Cat and I both need to get better at investigating cases without raising the community's suspicions. That pretty much means I have no time left for love or infatuation or whatever it was I once felt for Charles.

Anyway, who needs a boyfriend when you have a talking cat?

Not me. Well, at least not for right now.

Lately I've been spending a lot more time with my mom. Ever since she helped us catch the real murderer in our latest case, she's been on this kind of career high. She got the exclusive scoop and even managed to record our showdown with the murderer live and on camera. The feature was picked up all over the nation, and she and my dad have received job offers from clear across the country.

The latest was from San Antonio, I think.

She's not saying yes to any of them, though. At least, not unless I agree to move with them, too. But I would never leave Nan, and Nan would never leave Blueberry Bay.

So we're all staying put exactly where we are.

Sure, if enough people learn my secret, I probably will have to leave eventually. Right now, a total of five people know—Nan and my parents, who I told on purpose, along with Charles Longfellow, III and a college student named Mitch, who both figured it out by accident. Hopefully I can keep that number from growing any larger, but it seems like several people are on the verge of figuring things out already.

And that definitely worries me.

Especially since my mom just invited me to help her with her newest investigative journalism assignment...

I'd finally switched to a part-time schedule at the firm, and today was one of my days off. And by off, I meant I got to stay home and pack up my tiny rental house under the supervision of one very demanding tabby.

Not only did I have to discard a number of my belongings that he found to be inadequate, but he was also the reason I had to move in the first place. Granted, I'm the one who said I'd owe him a big favor if he allowed me to put him in a harness to take him outside. I hadn't counted on that favor amounting to more than six-thousand square feet, though.

As it turned out, the favor he wanted was for me to purchase the old manor house he had lived in with Ethel Fulton before she was murdered and, through a truly unbelievable series of events, he came to live with me. Now a twelve-dollar harness was costing me the better part of my five-thousand-dollar monthly stipend, and I'd learned to be more careful about promising my kitty companion open-ended favors.

Yes, my former boss, Richard Fulton, did offer me a generous break on the price. Also, there were fewer interested parties once the greater populace found that the former homeowner had been murdered, but still—*still!*—owning Fulton Manor would require a pretty penny from me not just to keep up with the mortgage, but also to carry out the many repairs that seemed to be more or less essential for safety purposes.

At least that's what the home inspector said.

Hardly any time has passed at all, and yet somehow the sale is final and the house is ready for me and Octo-Cat to move in. It's funny how bureaucracy can either slow things way down or speed them way up depending what side you approach the red tape from. Around Blueberry Bay, the Fultons owned the spool from which the red tape was unraveled, which meant I bought myself a manor house with very little effort on my part.

Nan, who adores both me and my cat in equal measure, decided to help out, too. Even though she'd owned her little Cape Cod style home for more than thirty-five years, she decided it was time to sell and move in with me at my new Eastern seaboard mansion.

"The difference is," she explained, "this time

I'll be living with you and not the other way around." That was how she justified kicking me out of her house less than a year ago, only to move in with me now.

Honestly, I'm more than a little thrilled to have an added buffer when it comes to Octo-Cat. I love him more than anything, but he also infuriates me on a regular basis, constantly finding new and exciting ways to push the poorly constructed boundaries I've tried to erect.

And so all of us are moving in this weekend, even though Nan hasn't even had an offer on her house yet. Breanne says it will be easier to sell without a current resident. Yes, I couldn't believe Nan hired Calhoun Realty to list her house, either. She and I needed to have a serious talk about family loyalty.

But first we had to survive the big move.

"Someone just pulled up outside," Octo-Cat informed me, hopping onto the end of the bed where the better part of my wardrobe was laid out for evaluation. I took packing as a good opportunity to downsize, even though my living space would increase nearly ten times.

A moment later an urgent knock sounded on

the front door and my mom's voice called out, "Angie? Angie, are you here?"

"Coming!" I yelled, letting the half-full box in my arms fall to the floor.

I flipped the deadbolt and my mom immediately pushed her way inside. "You'll never guess what happened!" she told me, reaching into my closet and grabbing one of my jackets, which she thrust at me excitedly.

"What?" I asked, still a bit sleepy and not quite ready for this level of enthusiasm.

She followed me into the kitchen where I grabbed a can of Diet Mountain Dew and flipped the tab. It was my latest attempt at a suitable coffee replacement, and so far, so good.

"Lou Harlow was murdered!" she squealed with delight.

"Um, Mom. How about a little less bliss over someone dying, please?" Lou Harlow wasn't just some random local, either. As one of the two senators appointed to represent the great state of Maine, she was one of the most famous people to reside in our little corner of Blueberry Bay.

And now she was dead. And for some reason, my mother was terribly excited about it.

"I'm sorry. I know it's sad she died and everything, but guess who's been asked to cover it?" She bit her lower lip and pointed both thumbs toward her chest while widening her eyes to a comical degree.

"Congrats," I murmured, still feeling icky about her reaction to this whole thing.

"Thank you," she said with an airy smile. "Turns out I did such a great job covering the Hayes murders, the station would like me to do another investigative piece."

"I'm really happy for you, Mom." And I was. She'd worked hard to get here, and at last everything was coming up... bodies in the morgue, I guess.

"Good, because I need you to do it with me."

"What? No, no, no, no." Yeah, I'd done the legwork to find the Hayes's real killer and clear Brock Calhoun's name, but that didn't mean I wanted to jump straight into another murder investigation, especially one as prominent as this one would no doubt prove to be.

"Angie, I don't really think you have a choice."

I groaned and shook my head. "Oh, yeah, because that's the way to win me over."

"The senator was killed in her home," she revealed. "Do you know where that home is?"

"Somewhere in Glendale?" I guessed with a sigh.

"Not just somewhere," my mom corrected with a new light dancing in her hazel eyes. "Right next door to your new house."

CHAPTER TWO

Well, this was exactly *not* what I needed on moving day. My new home had already been tainted by murder, and now the place next door had become an active crime scene as well.

My mom stared at me with wide, sparkling eyes. "Well?" She nudged me with her elbow as if we were doing something as harmless as discussing reality TV gossip. This wasn't reality TV, though. It was actually real life. *My life.*

"I know that look," Octo-Cat proclaimed from his seat beside me. "It's the same one you get right before you decide to do something stupid."

"Well, good luck on the investigation," I mumbled, hoping to silence them both so I could get back to packing.

It didn't work.

My mom grabbed both my wrists and attempted to drag me from my chair. "Come with me. I need you," she whined, drawing out each word dramatically. No wonder she'd become Blueberry Bay's go-to newswoman. Even I found myself both wanting and dreading to know what would happen next.

I yanked my arms away and wrapped them around my waist defensively. "In case you forgot, it's my moving day, and I still have lots to do before the movers get here in a few hours."

Mom baulked at this excuse as she moved behind my chair and put a hand on each of my shoulders, causing me to flinch. "A few hours? Why, that's way more than enough time to take a quick glance. Besides, aren't you curious?"

I bit my lip and tried really hard not to say anything. The truth was I had, in fact, begun to enjoy the thrill of the investigation. And despite my better judgment and bigger priorities, I was definitely intrigued by the newest murder in town having happened right next door to my new place.

A fresh corpse next door. What a housewarming gift!

Seeing that she had me on the hook, Mom

began to reel me in. She put her face beside mine and tipped my chair back. "Tell you what. How about you come with me now and, after we take a quick look-see, I'll come back to help you finish packing. Deal?"

I groaned and pressed my forehead to the table. The chair's front legs landed back on the floor with a jarring thud. "Deal," I murmured into the cold wood.

"Right back into the thick of it. Why am I not surprised?" Octo-Cat commented drolly before trotting off without so much as a glance my way.

"Yay!" My mom clapped her hands several times and began to yank on my arm again. Sometimes I felt like the most grown up person in my entire family, which was saying something since Mom was in her early fifties and Nan had already high-tailed it well past seventy.

"Let's go," Mom said, tugging at my arm once again. This time I got up and followed. "I'll fill you in on what I know on our drive over."

True to her word, the moment the car doors closed beside us, my mom jammed her key in the ignition and started to talk. "I know you were never interested in politics too much, but Lou Harlow was a four term senator. She won every term by a huge landslide and was probably going to be re-elected the next time, too. Everyone around here loved her, which makes her death all the more shocking."

I chewed on my thumbnail as she spoke, a bad habit that had gotten more and more out of control lately.

My mom swatted me with one of her perfectly manicured hands. "Stop that. It's gross!"

"Sorry," I muttered, running my index finger across my jagged thumbnail as I switched my focus back to the matter at hand. "So, a political rival wanted her seat and it was easier to murder her than to try to win fair and square?"

"Maybe," my mom said, bringing both hands back to the steering wheel now that she'd decided she didn't need to hit me a second time. "We'll definitely work that angle and see what we come up with."

I sensed a *but*. When Mom didn't provide it, I decided to give her the lead in. "But?"

"Why kill her at home when she spends most of her time in Washington?" she asked as if I might actually have the answer.

I shrugged. "Maybe it was more convenient."

"It's too obvious, though. Don't you think?" She frowned as she considered this.

"Well, maybe our killer isn't very smart. How did the senator die, anyway?" In my experience, killers usually were pretty smart, actually. Smart, but vain. Combine those two traits with their lack of a moral compass, and it often spelled trouble—both for their victims and for me, the fiery upstart who did my best to help bring them to justice.

Well, lately, at least.

Would I continue chasing killers around Blueberry Bay forever?

Only time would tell, but I had a sneaking suspicion that the answer just might be a resounding *Oh, heck yeah!*

Mom pulled up to a stop sign and switched on her blinker, then turned to look at me. Once again, her expression was filled with utter joy as she revealed, "Somebody pushed her down the stairs!"

Oh, for the love of…

"Then how do they know it wasn't just some stupid accident?" It looked like we might have both gotten ahead of ourselves, and here I was considering myself the sleuth of the century—at least as far as Glendale, Maine was concerned.

Mom seemed flustered. *"They?* Who's they? We are the ones investigating this, and we don't know for sure, but we definitely suspect foul play."

I bit my tongue to keep from mentioning that the police were still the true detectives here and that I was too new to the case to be a part of her royal *we*. It seemed I still had to learn this lesson for myself, too.

Shaking off my disappointment, I turned my head to watch the scenery flying past my window. Greenery stretched as far as the eye could see— trees, flowers, grass, everywhere life. Well, except at Lou Harlow's manor house.

Gulls drifted on the breeze, reminding me that gorgeous Blueberry Bay was just beyond the horizon. We lived so close to the ocean that the air always tasted slightly of salt. My new house sat so close to the shoreline, in fact, that I could walk there in ten minutes flat.

"I really wish people would stop turning up dead around here," I told my mom with a sigh. We were a small town to begin with. If the murders continued at their current clip, we'd be down half our population by the end of next year.

"Don't you think it's just a little bit exciting?" my mom said as she navigated us down the private drive that served all the most elite homes in Glendale—including now, rather inexplicably, *mine.*

I understood where my mom was coming from, though. For years, she'd wasted her journalistic talents on puff pieces and human interest stories. This new dastardly turn of events in our small town made for big news and a far more interesting job for her.

Still, people were dying, and that was definitely a problem.

I was saved from answering her question by the appearance of red and blue flashing lights on the top of the hill. My mom drove one turnoff past my new house and pulled right up to the late Lou Harlow's estate. Cops were everywhere, definitely more than technically worked for our sleepy little town. It seemed as if the whole county had arrived—whether to help investigate or merely to gawk remained to be seen.

A few officers stood by the entryway chatting over takeout coffees. Others paraded around the property talking into their radios and trying to look important. Somebody else worked on stretching that jarring yellow crime scene tape around the porch.

I hated it. I hated it so much. The good senator deserved better than this. We all did.

Mom pulled straight up behind the nearest cop car and shut of the engine. "Ready?" she asked with a quick glance my way before charging out of the car and right over to the group of officers who had gathered by the house.

"Quite the scene you've got here," she said jovially while I struggled to catch up. Even though I was taller than my mom and should have had a quicker stride, she'd always buzzed around like a hummingbird, sometimes moving so fast you could scarcely keep track.

"Yeah, and it's a private one at that," a county officer informed us both, making a little shooing gesture with her hand.

"Laura Lee, Channel 7 News," Mom answered proudly, shoving a hand forward in greeting.

The officer sneered and refused to take the proffered hand. "Oh, then we definitely don't want you here."

One of our local boys spotted us from across the yard and shouted, "It's okay. She's with us." Officer Bouchard jogged over to join us. "She's got the needed clearance," he told the others.

"Thank you," my mom said, simpering at the county officer who had tried to deny our access. "Now, be a dear and catch us up, please."

I sighed and made a mental note that *How to Win Friends & Influence People* would be the perfect gift for my mom on the next holiday that required such things.

"Officer Raines?" my mom read from the angry lady cop's badge. "I just want to help."

"Like heck you do," the other one spat back.

I tried to block their bickering out as I studied the massive stone façade before us. Just like my new house—Fulton Manor—this one was at least five-thousand square feet and probably about as old as the state of Maine itself. Gorgeous bay windows stuck out at odd intervals around the second floor in what appeared to be a recent remodeling job. I wondered if you could see the ocean from up there. Whatever the case, they seemed like nice little nooks to hang out with a good book. Maybe I could add a window seat as part of my own remodels as well.

I'd almost fully immersed myself in this book-worm fantasy of mine when a flash of something caught my eye. I squinted to try to make out what was up there, but was met only with the fluttering of drapes. Whoever or whatever was looking out upon the chaotic scene below had now disappeared.

I left mom to continue her battle with Officer Raines and inched slowly toward the entry. Her preferred method of investigation may have been talking, but I'd always preferred to jump straight in with both feet and see what I could discover.

At least if I found trouble waiting for me on the inside, I knew there were a dozen-odd officers loitering nearby. Any of them could offer up some help in a pinch.

See?

I had nothing to worry about as I tiptoed right into the middle of this fresh crime scene.

CHAPTER THREE

Despite the flurry of activity outside, the inside of the manor house sat empty—eerily so. As soon as I entered, I came face to face with the grand staircase. It had been cordoned off and the area was already scrubbed clean, though the recent disturbance was obvious.

One of the lower steps had caved in on itself, calling into question the soundness of the entire structure. A few feet from the landing, the body position had been marked in a shining white outline. *The poor senator.* She'd been a huge force in life, but the outline marking her death seemed impossibly small.

As much as my mother assumed I didn't know about the political scene or about current events in general, I'd actually voted for the senator in her two most recent elections. She'd fought hard to protect the natural beauty of our great country and the citizens within it. Even though I liked to think of myself as non-partisan, I agreed with Senator Lou Harlow's stances more often than not.

Plus, from the few televised interviews or online news articles I'd managed to catch, I liked her. She reminded me of Nan, but in a tailored pant suit instead of a flowy silk kimono.

She'd done so much tireless work on behalf of the people, and now one of those people had killed her. I bowed my head and said a quick prayer, hoping that her death had happened quickly and without pain, and that the killer would soon be brought to justice.

I'd been around murder a lot lately, but somehow this one felt more personal. Lou Harlow wasn't a stranger. She was someone I'd seen on the TV, the Internet, and even the odd newspaper that still found its way into the firm where I worked.

"There you are," Mom shouted after me, disturbing the sanctity of the moment as she flew in through the open front door.

I kept my eyes fixed straight ahead. Was there some important clue I'd missed because emotions were clouding my judgment with this one?

"Such a shame," Mom clucked, finally showing a blessed bit of remorse.

We stood side by side, studying the scene. A glint of yellowish green at the top of the stairs drew my eye and I stepped forward to get a better look.

"What is it? What do you see?" Mom asked in an excited whisper.

I still hadn't figured out what was up there, but I pointed anyway.

We both craned our heads and shifted our angles until finally I saw a scary, mummy-looking face watching me from above. "It's some kind of animal, I think." Although it looked like none I'd ever come across before. Maybe in a zoo, but in the wilds of coastal Maine? I think not.

"The senator did have two pet cats," Mom pointed out, still struggling and twisting in an effort to discern the animal for herself.

"Whatever's up there, I'm not really sure it's a cat." I took another step forward, bending my neck straight back to achieve a fresh perspective.

All that did was hurt me, though. "*Ugh.* I wish it wasn't so dark in here," I moaned.

Mom lifted her phone high and then snapped a picture of the area using her flash. The burst of light was more than enough to fully illuminate that same little animal that had first caught my eye. A second larger one of the same kind also sat farther back away from the bannister. They still looked like something that had come straight out of a horror movie, but now at least I could clearly tell they were cats.

Cats with no fur and lots of wrinkles. *Eww.*

I shuddered as I pictured Octo-Cat shorn down in a similar fashion, and that particular mental image was even scarier than the two odd Sphynxes sitting before me.

Mom showed me the picture she'd managed to get on her phone. "They're hairless cats," she said matter-of-factly.

I shivered again. "Why would anyone want a cat without hair?"

"Allergies? Attention?" Mom guessed and offered me a casual shrug. "Could have been either with the Senator."

A growl sounded above, and I swear the little hairs on the back of my neck shot straight up. I was a newly branded cat person, so why did these two freak me out so much? Was it that they were hairless or that they were staked out at a murder scene? Both?

After another emphatic growl, the larger of the two cats appeared at the top of the stairs, peering down at us like a dissatisfied overlord. Or a prison guard. Or a killer.

"Hi," I said, even though I knew he couldn't understand me without Octo-Cat here to translate.

He opened his mouth wide, then let out a terrible hiss before turning tail and stalking off with the smaller cat in pursuit.

"I am officially terrified of those things," I said.

Mom shoved her phone back into her bag and turned to me with that same excited expression she'd worn most of the morning. "Know what I'm thinking?"

"I'm not sure I want to know," I admitted. I should have been at home packing the last of my boxes for the big move, not shaking in my flip flops at the sight of these two bizarre felines. There was absolutely no reason this little investigation of ours couldn't have waited.

Mom grabbed my hand and gave it a squeeze. Obviously, we were not thinking the same thing here. "I'm thinking," she revealed with a happy squeal, "that this looks like a job for Pet Whisperer, P.I."

"Pet Whisperer? P.I.?" I shook my head and tried very hard not to roll my eyes. Of course, she'd given me a special headline-worthy moniker. She'd probably already written and rewritten my featured story in her head several times over.

"That's your new name," she said, squeezing my hand again. "Do you like it?"

"Um, I'm fine just being Angie." *Must not encourage this.* I wanted my special ability to remain a secret, not become front page news.

"Not for you," Mom said with a sigh. "For your business."

"I don't have a business," I pointed out. I still didn't like where she was headed with all of this.

"Wrong again," she crooned. "You're already doing the work. You might as well hang out your sign and get paid for it."

"Interesting idea, but I don't want people to know I can talk to animals," I reminded her. Besides, I still had my part-time salary from the law firm and my full-time stipend for being Octo-

Cat's official guardian and the overseer of his trust fund.

"Everyone will think it's a gimmick," Mom countered with a wink. "But only we'll know the truth. Besides, it will give you an excuse to bring your cat with you while investigating, which is what you need anyway, right? I mean, if he'd been here this morning, we could have cracked the whole case wide open by now. Those cats definitely know what happened. I just know it."

"Why do you have to be so excited about this?" I asked, resigned to the fact that I was apparently opening a business now—and, worse still, that my cat would be my new business partner.

"That's branding, baby," Mom answered with a glamorous flip of her hair.

Oh, brother. Or rather—*oh, mother.*

I took a couple big steps back, careful not to upset the crime scene as I walked away from the crazy lady who just so happened to be my mother. Turning to the door now, I said, "Okay, great. So, I'm just going to go make sure the police know the cats are up there. With the stairs cordoned off, it might not be easy to get them down."

Mom followed after me as I returned to the

bright world outside. I squinted from the sudden onslaught of sunniness and swept my eyes over the premises in search of the one officer I knew well enough to approach. Once my eyes adjusted to the light again, I spotted Officer Bouchard at the edge of the property examining a small copse of evergreens at the edge of a much larger deciduous forest that divided Harlow's property from mine.

I jogged over to him, knowing my mom would have no trouble keeping up if she wanted to.

"Did you know there are cats inside?" I asked him, embarrassed by the fact my breaths came out labored from that short burst of exercise.

"That would be Jacques and Jillianne," he said with a chuckle. "Ugly little things, aren't they?"

"They're… cute. Um, in a different way," I insisted. In a *very* different way. Still, even though I'd just had the same thought myself, I suddenly felt defensive on their behalf.

My mom joined us then, having chosen to stroll elegantly across the field rather than run like I did. I guess it was now part of her persona or something. *The news waits for no man,* she'd often told me, *but for a woman, it just might.*

Officer Bouchard smiled kindly at Mom. "Yeah. The senator picked them up from a breeder in France, thus the fancy names. They're slippery little buggers, too. I've been trying to catch them all morning, but so far, no luck. Figure with the next of kin on the way, the cats can be his problem when he gets here."

"Next of kin?" Mom inserted herself between me and him. She'd already pulled out her phone and started the recording app, which she now held up to him like a microphone. "And who might that be?"

Officer Bouchard stared at the phone, then cleared his throat and answered in a crisp, clear voice, "Her son, Matthew Harlow. Lives in Chicago. Should be here by nightfall."

"And who do you think killed Lou Harlow?" Mom asked, pressing the phone even closer to his face.

He sighed and pushed her hand aside. "I think it's too soon to say. We haven't even ruled out the possibility of it being an accident yet."

Until today, I'd only seen one crime scene before—Bill and Ruth Hayes, who were murdered in their own home. I saw it long after the fact, but I'd had the same feeling today as I'd had then.

Call it my gut.

Call it intuition.

Or maybe even just a lucky guess.

Whatever the case, I knew it had been no accident that killed Lou Harlow. Someone had wanted her dead and decided to take matters into his or her own hands.

Now we just had to figure out who.

The Pet Whisperer P.I. was officially on the case.

CHAPTER FOUR

As promised, Mom stuck around to help me finish my packing and, as much as it pained me to admit, I almost wished she wouldn't have. For starters, she had an opinion on *everything*.

I'm not exaggerating either. *Everything*.

As she picked up each of my possessions one by one, she frowned and turned them over in her hands. Apparently she believed that if she studied my things from all angles, they might suddenly transform into something that would match her expectations.

Growing up, I had often wondered if she felt the same way about me, but now I knew better. Mom was a nice lady and I know she loved me as best she could, but she had most definitely not been cut from the divine maternal cloth.

"Do you really need to take this with you?" she asked me now. "I can get you a newer one. A better one."

After about an hour of this same conversation over and over again, she'd basically promised to buy me a new life as part of my housewarming gift. I know our tastes didn't match up—Mom was far more sophisticated than I'd ever be—but still, it would have been nice for her to give it a rest.

The other problem I had just then was that I desperately wanted to discuss the crime scene and those weird Sphynx cats with Octo-Cat. Yes, even though Mom knew I could talk to him, it still felt weird to carry on a conversation right there in front of her.

Our tastes weren't the only thing that differed. Mom was all cold, hard facts and evidence. She'd ask a million and one questions, including many I wouldn't know how to answer. Namely, *how come you two can talk to each other?*

I still had no idea why Octo-Cat and I had formed this connection or even really how it worked. One day I'd love to figure all that out, but I was too busy with my move at present to sit around and speculate all the many possibilities with my mom.

"You know," Mom said as she studied the plates and bowls stacked in one of my kitchen cupboards. "You're going to be living in a manor house now. A lot of your things don't really match that aesthetic. It may be jarring for visitors."

"It's fine, Mom," I said, nudging her out of the way with my hip and packing away the offensive dishes myself. "I don't really plan on having a lot of visitors, and I'm not really the hoity toity type. You know that about me."

She stepped to the side and opened another cabinet. "Maybe there's a middle ground here," she insisted. "Nan has a nice set of dinnerware. You could throw yours out and stick with hers instead. Oh! Or you could donate yours. You love those charity shops, right?"

"Maybe," I said to acknowledge the topic so that we could both move on. I did like the thrift shops, but I much preferred buying from them over donating my own things.

Mom frowned, and I hugged one of my cheery red plates to my chest. I liked my plates, and I liked my life, too. Why couldn't Mom just accept that she and I were never going to see eye to eye on certain issues? So what if most of the things in my kitchen came from the dollar store? They all worked just as well as the things Mom bought for a hundred times the price at her fancy chain boutiques.

"Oh, I like these," she said, staring into the next cupboard over as she grabbed a floral-patterned Lennox teacup and studied it with wide eyes.

"I don't want her messing with my stuff," Octo-Cat informed me, hopping up onto the counter and giving Mom such a startle, she dropped the much admired teacup right onto the ground.

The three of us watched what followed in slow motion, but it was already, regrettably too late. The delicate cup burst into smithereens and Octo-Cat let out an ear-piercing cry. "My Evian vessel!"

Mom took a step back. "I'm so sorry," she told me, and I could tell she genuinely meant it. Maybe she picked at me not to be mean, but just because she sometimes had a hard time thinking of other things to discuss. Maybe that was why she got so excited over sharing the Lou Harlow murder investigation with me.

"I'll get you a new set, I promise," she said, blinking back tears. Suddenly, I felt like the absolute worst daughter in the world. Why did I have such difficulty spending more than a few minutes at a time in my mom's company? I'd need to try harder.

Of course, I didn't have the heart to tell her that this particular set was irreplaceable. They'd belonged to Octo-Cat's previous owner, the late Ethel Fulton, and they were one of the few things he still had left of her. Granted, we'd soon be moving into her mostly furnished manor home, but still. This tea set had been special to Octo-Cat. It was the only way he'd take his food or water, and now that he was down a cup, I'd have to increase my dish-washing schedule to boot.

"Look," I said, trying to be as gentle as possible. "I think I can handle things from here. Why don't you go see what else you can find out about the Harlow murder?"

She twisted her hands anxiously. "Are you sure?" Despite her hesitation, I could tell she was just as eager to go as I was to have her leave.

Did I feel guilty? *Sure.* I'd probably never stop feeling guilty when it came to my strained relationship with her and Dad.

Still, Mom and I had always gotten along best in brief bursts. I loved that we were becoming closer these last few weeks, but we needed more time to navigate our new relationship—and this really wasn't the best day for us to put in the work, as calloused as that sounded even to my own ear.

It just couldn't be a priority with all the other things I needed to do.

I side-stepped the broken teacup and gave my mom a tight hug. "I'm sure. I can tell you're dying to get back on the case. I'll be fine here."

Mom sighed happily. *"Mmm,* you know me so well," she said before quickly gathering her things and racing toward the door. "I'll text with any updates. Bye!"

And just like that, she was gone again.

Octo-Cat resumed his agonized mewling. Even though we could understand each other, sometimes he still reverted to the classic cat sounds—usually in periods of intense emotion —like now.

"I'm sorry," I told him, carefully stroking his head. I hoped it would offer comfort and also that the kindly gesture would not result in me getting bitten, but you kind of never knew with Octo-Cat.

"It's like Ethel just died all over again," he told

me. His ears twitched then fell flat against his head. His tail swished back and forth like a metronome. His eyes grew so wide and dark that I was sure he would have cried, were such a trait in his biology.

"I'm really sorry," I told him again, unsure of what else I could do.

He stared at the tiny fragments of Lennox that lay scattered across the kitchen floor. Whites, pinks, gold-trimmed, all nothing more than broken pieces of the life he'd once known. Great. Now I was tearing up, too.

"I'll just go get the broom," I mumbled, not wanting him to see how moved I now was on his behalf.

But before I could turn away, Octo-Cat shot out in front of me and screamed, "No!"

My heart beat ratcheted up a few notches, thumping wildly as I wondered what crazy thing my cat might do next. "Whoa, what happened?"

"I'm just not ready yet," he informed me. "I need some time with it first."

"With the broken teacup?" I asked gently. He'd gotten better at detecting sarcasm and punished me whenever he heard it in my voice or saw it on my face. He was allowed to talk to me however he pleased, of course, but I had to maintain the utmost respect at all times.

Even times like this.

Octo-Cat sniffed and lifted his nose high as he did whenever he wanted to appear superior. "Yes," he answered simply.

"Unfortunately, we don't really have time." I kept my face placid, understanding. "The movers will be here in an hour or so. And we can't keep stepping around the mess. It's dangerous. One of us could cut a foot on those sharp shards."

He let out a mournful meow, then turned away. "Do as you must."

I resumed my journey to get the broom and dustpan, feeling like the worst cat owner in the world. That made me the worst daughter and the worst cat owner all within the span of about ten minutes. My stock would not be rising anytime soon.

When I returned, Octo-Cat still stood frozen in that dramatic pose of his. Normally, his antics bugged me, but at that moment, I truly felt sorry for him and his loss.

"Would it help if we said a few words?" I suggested.

The morose tabby turned his head slightly

and peered at me from the corners of his eyes. "Like a funeral?"

"Yeah," I said with a shrug. "Like a funeral."

He shifted the rest of the way out of his pose and faced me straight on. Already he looked better, like his heart had started to piece itself back together. "Where will we bury it?" he wanted to know.

"Oh. *Umm.*" I did not have time for this, but he also seemed sincere and in need of closure, so I suggested something I hoped would suit us both. "We should bury it tonight at Ethel's." That would buy me the time I needed to pack at least, and hopefully it would make him feel better about this whole episode, too.

"Great idea, Angela," Octo-Cat said with one of his hard-earned smiles.

I glowed in the light of his rare and wonderful praise. He was a diva, sure, but it did feel good to make him happy, especially considering that most of the time every little thing I did disappointed him greatly.

"*Tonight,*" he shouted merrily. "That also gives me time to work on what I'll say." He then trotted off, leaving me to tidy the mess and prepare it for burial.

Ugh. As glad as I was that he felt better, I'd planned to talk to him about Lou Harlow's murder and the strange cats she'd left behind.

Well, that would just have to wait.

Why was my to do list only getting longer the harder I worked today?

CHAPTER FIVE

All of Octo-Cat's previous sorrow evaporated the moment we pulled into the long, winding driveway of Fulton Manor.

"Home!" he yowled, even being so brave as to detach his claws from my thigh so he could prop himself up and look out the window. "Oh, it feels so good to be home!"

I parked and opened my driver's side door, and he immediately jumped over me to get to the ground outside. "Home!" he continued to cry as he rolled back and forth in the grass like a crazy kitty.

I was just about to ask him to rein it in when he raced up the porch steps and through his specialty cat door, which slid open in response to a special signal his collar emitted. All this time I'd never replaced his collar and he'd never asked me to. He probably always knew we'd end up here someday. After all, he'd engineered the entire thing.

Octo-Cat had clearly found a way to keep himself occupied. Meanwhile, the movers were still packing things up at my old rental, which gave me a little bit of time alone with my new mansion now.

A mansion! And it belonged to me!

Ridiculous.

But, okay, also super cool.

My eyes moved up the three stories all the way to the turret rising up beyond the far side of the roof. I'd already decided to make my bedroom there in the tippity top tower just like some kind of weirdo modern-day princess. Nan had claimed the master bedroom, which had belonged to Ethel before she died. It was also where she had died, and I just felt icky about being in the same house, let alone the very same bedroom.

Nan simply laughed and said, "Oh, sweetie pie. Death is a part of life." I figured at her advanced age, it must not bother her as much as it did me. Personally, I hoped I never reached the point in life where I was comfortable sleeping in the same spot a dead body had lain only months before.

It was eerie enough moving into a house that had served as the scene of a murder. In fact, I was still working on coming to terms with it. By now, I felt pretty sure my first electric bill would be many hundreds of dollars, seeing as I planned to sleep with every single light on until I no longer felt afraid of my own house.

Had it been my choice, I'd never have picked a dwelling so grand. But Octo-Cat had insisted upon it. Even Mr. Fulton—my former boss— seemed happy to be unloading the house quickly, even at a substantial loss to himself and the other heirs.

As I watched Octo-Cat run back and forth through the cat door, moaning with delight each and every time, I really did have to admit the place suited him. So what if he was a common housecat? Looks could be deceiving, and his heart was definitely bourgeois to the max.

I left him to his merriment and grabbed one of the lighter boxes from my trunk. Inside, a thin veil of dust clung to almost every possible surface. I probably should have cleaned it out before moving in, but I didn't exactly have the cash to hire someone. Besides, the move had happened so suddenly, I barely had time to pack, let alone do much of anything else.

We'd get to it. Eventually.

Just add it to the bottom of my never-ending to do list. Or maybe somewhere in the middle.

My goal was to have the place at least livable before Nan joined us at the end of the month. She needed more time to pack up the entire life she'd lived in Blueberry Bay as well as all her mementos from her time on Broadway.

I understood that, so I didn't tell her how the thought of sleeping in this giant place alone frightened me to the very core. I had Octo-Cat, who may or may not protect me in the event of danger. A fifty-fifty shot was still better than having zero help, if the need for it were to suddenly occur.

Another unsettling thing?

Fulton Manor and Harlow Manor next door had almost the exact same blueprint. Although they were both built well before the rise of the McMansion, I guess somebody had liked the first so much, they'd decided to build a second almost exactly like it.

Somehow, I found myself drifting toward the grand staircase time and again. It looked so much like the one next door that it made me shudder each time I passed. I was like a deranged moth drawn right into the middle of the flame. *Burn, baby, burn.*

"What's wrong with you?" my cat asked, eyeing me wearily after his ten-millionth time through the cat door.

I shrugged. "Just a bit weirded out by the murder next door."

He stopped dead in his tracks, not even putting his front left paw all the way down as he stared at me. "Wait, *what?* Somebody killed that nice old lady? When?"

Oh, that was right. We hadn't gotten the chance to talk yet, given the entire teacup episode. "This morning," I told him, watching him carefully to see how he'd react once he had more information. "Or, probably last night, actually."

He gasped and stomped his paw down onto the hardwood floor. "And you didn't tell me?"

"There was that whole thing with the teacup, and I… I'm sorry." I apologized, knowing that it was the most surefire way to avoid an altercation. Octo-Cat loved fighting and hated losing, which meant I was constantly on the bum end of *that* deal.

He shook his head in dismay and stared at me for an uncomfortably long time before trotting up a few stairs and positioning himself just so. "Go on. Tell me now," he demanded. "I need to know exactly what happened."

I felt nervous under the spotlight of his scrutinous gaze but did as I was told. For as much as he was supposed to be my pet, it really felt as if I were the one who'd been trained. "The senator was killed. Someone pushed her down the staircase," I explained.

"The staircase!" Octo-Cat exclaimed, lifting one paw and then the other while he stared at the stoop beneath him.

I nodded dumbly, unable to form words just then.

"Jacques and Jillianne," he somehow managed to hiss between clenched teeth. "I'll skin them alive, those good for nothings." He jogged down the steps and was just about to dart out the cat door again before I stopped him.

"Wait!" I cried. "You know Jacques and Jillianne?" I felt so stupid every time I said their Frenchified names. Why did cats need such fancy names? Octo-Cat was bad enough with his eight names, but at least all of them were in English. Wait. They were, right? It was honestly kind of hard to remember, thus his new and improved— and much, much shorter—moniker.

He sighed but kept his back to me. His tiny kitty shoulders heaved with the weight of his obvious disappointment in me. "Of course I know them. We used to live next door and—will you look at that?—now we do again."

"Are you friends?" I asked eagerly, running a half circle around him so that we were once again face to face.

He looked like he was about to sneeze. He didn't. Instead, he said, "With those weirdos? No way."

"I mean, they look a little different, but that's not a reason to—"

"It's not their looks, Angela. It's the way they talk." He growled at me, much like the big hairless cat had that morning.

I wasn't sure what game we were playing here, but I hated to be left out. I shook my head and scowled at him. "You're not sounding any less racist here. Or is it breedist? Whatever the case, not a shining moment from you."

He simply chuckled. "Oh, you'll see what I mean. Give it some time. Shouldn't take too long."

He trotted up a few steps and then turned back to me, something I couldn't quite interpret shining in his eyes. "By the way," he said as if a sudden thought had just occurred to him.

"Death by staircase? Yeah, classic cat move."

"What do you—?" I started.

He cut me off with a villainous laugh he liked to trot out whenever he wanted to be particularly theatrical. Apparently, this was one of those blessed times.

"I mean," he said, between manic gasps for air. "Jacques and Jillianne killed your senator. The cats are guilty. Case closed." He sulked slowly away, still laughing to himself.

I took two giant steps back, feeling like I'd just looked into the void and saw my death play out before my very eyes. Whatever happened next, I'd make sure to watch my step when it came to the grand staircase I'd once considered the crowning feature of my new home.

Octo-Cat's laughter echoed through the halls. Why was this so funny to him? Why was he still laughing, and about this?

Apparently, he and my mom shared the same morbid fascination with the senator's death. Too bad they both talked to me instead of each other.

It's just his way, I reminded myself. *He likes being the center of attention. He'd never actually hurt you.*

But then I thought of all those little old cat ladies who died in the city only to be devoured by their most beloved pets and shuddered again...

Well, at least I knew Octo-Cat would only eat Fancy Feast.

CHAPTER SIX

Even though I needed to take some items upstairs, I decided to stick to the main level of the house while the movers hauled all my heaviest belongings in through the front door. I'd need just a little bit more time to come to grips with what Octo-Cat had just revealed about feline-on-human homicide and the preferred method for it.

Here I hadn't even known such a horror existed. *Silly me.*

Truth be told, I hadn't brought much from my old place, and so my preliminary unpacking was quick. Since I still felt queasy every time I passed by the staircase, I decided to head outside and take a walk around the property.

Gorgeous, intricately kept flowerbeds

surrounded the house on three sides, and the back opened up to a lovely two-tiered deck, complete with a fire pit and twin porch swings. Farther out, a thick forest rimmed the property, giving it all the privacy you could want and more.

Okay, so half my week would probably now be spent on yard maintenance going forward, but even I had to admit it would be time well spent.

A soft rumble in the distance along with a flash of red between the trees caught my eye, and I tromped through the grass to check it out. Apparently, if I angled my head just right, I could see straight through to the late senator's yard. A bright red sports car had just pulled up the drive, and it was one I recognized instantly. After all, there were only two fancy red sports cars in all of Glendale; Nan drove one while Thompson owned the other.

I watched in horror as my boss, the senior partner at our law firm, Mr. Richard Thompson, clambered out of his car and up the steps toward the house. Uncharacteristically, he came without the briefcase that was usually attached to him like a boxy extension of his left limb. He also appeared nervous as he loosened his tie and glanced around the estate to see if anyone else was nearby. The police had mostly cleared out by then—or at least taken their get-together elsewhere. And, thank goodness, he didn't know to search for me on the other side of the forest.

I remained rooted to the spot as Officer Bouchard stepped out of the house and strode forward to greet Mr. Thompson. His badge reflected the sunshine like a polished nickel. "Richard, can I help you with something?"

I craned my neck to try to make out Mr. Thompson's expression, but a low-hanging branch blocked my view.

"I heard the news," Thompson said. His deep voice projected through the forest. "Thought I'd stop by to pay my respects."

Officer Bouchard jogged down the steps and motioned for the other man to follow. "I'm sure you don't need me to tell you that this isn't the appropriate time or place."

"I know," my boss agreed. He seemed unsure of what to do with his hands. "It was just so... so unexpected."

The policeman sighed and raised one of his arms high to run a hand through his hair. "Yeah, we're all pretty beat up about this one. It doesn't change the rules, though."

They exchanged a few quiet words that got lost before they reached my ears, and then Mr. Thompson climbed back into his car and left.

"What was *that* about?" Octo-Cat asked, choosing that exact moment to rub up against my leg and giving me the fright of my life.

"I have no idea," I told him honestly, still very much suspicious as to how both me and my firm at large now became tangled up in every single murder around town. Granted, there weren't any murders until Ethel Fulton earlier this year—or at least none that I knew about.

"I hope somebody without any pets moves in next," he informed me with a bored yawn as we both stared vacantly through the trees.

This surprised me enough to risk a glance toward him. It's not like anything was happening at Harlow Manor anymore. Even Officer Bouchard had disappeared from view now.

"Don't you like other cats?" I asked him.

"In *my* territory?" He made a sarcastic *psshaw* noise. "I'd much rather *not* share, if given the choice. This is my land. These are my trees to climb, and in their branches? Those are my birds to devour… or at least deliver to the foot of your bed when you've been a good human."

I shuddered at the memory of his most recent *gift*. "I guess I'll make sure not to be a good human then."

He nipped at the blades of grass in front of his paws, swallowed a few bites, and then snickered. "Just for that, now my puke will be green."

"Um, okay," I said with a shrug. Honestly, his punishments often weren't much worse than his rewards, and this one seemed especially tame.

"It will throw off your whole day," he explained with a smirk. His laughter became sinister, and I knew he'd gone full-on into evil genius mode. The only problem with that is our definitions of the word *genius* varied substantially.

When he stopped laughing, he took a deep breath and glanced up at me. "You don't get it, do you?" he said with a frustrated groan that was also part growl.

I shook my head, just as Officer Bouchard popped into view outside of the Harlow place. Why was he there? What was he doing?

"You'll have to clean up green puke," my cat explained between laughs that seemed to be losing their steam. "Normally, you start your day by cleaning up brown puke. You see? It will make everything different right from the start of your day. You won't be able to stand it!"

"You got me," I said with a resigned sigh. It would be better for us both if he thought he'd found a new means of punishing me. He derived such great pleasure from trying out new training techniques, that I didn't have the heart to correct his misunderstandings when it came to what did and didn't work for disciplining humans.

"Got it out of your system now?" I asked, turning back to study him with a skeptical smile.

"For now," he answered. "But just you wait until tomorrow morning!"

"Okay, great." I glanced back toward Officer Bouchard's immovable form and my curiosity continued to grow. Who would kill a four term senator when she was so liked by her constituents? Why did the police find it necessary to guard the crime scene? And what, if anything, did her weird, hairless cats have to do with it all?

"Hey, are you busy right now?" I asked my cat when I realized he might be able to sneak through the woods for a closer look.

He just turned his nose up and said, "Yes," then turned around with his tail also held high in the air, flashing me an unnecessary view of his kitty butt.

"Well, thanks for that," I shouted after him.

With one more glance though the trees, I decided to give it a rest. At least for now. Maybe the cops had already identified the culprit and that's why they were guarding the scene. Even if I had an official title now as part of Mom's impromptu branding session this morning, I was still inexperienced and new at this.

The police were the experts, and I had to trust them to do their jobs right. Even as I thought those words, however, I knew it would only be a matter of time before I found myself creeping through those trees to investigate the scene of the murder firsthand.

CHAPTER SEVEN

Night was fast approaching by the time the movers left. They not only helped me move my meager belongings in, but they also stayed to help reorganize the existing furniture within the manor and to pack some of the unneeded pieces into their truck for a quick stop off to the local charity shop.

Okay, maybe not so quick, considering they ended up moving more out than they moved in. But I definitely wasn't keeping the bed Ethel had died in, or any of her bedroom set for that matter. I didn't care that Nan was just fine repurposing the furniture for her own use. Tt creeped me out and I refused to keep any part of it in my home. It was already bad enough that Octo-Cat absolutely refused to part with the formal dining room set that had hosted the poisonous dinner party. I did not need to top that off with my Nan sleeping in some other old lady's death bed.

"I'm glad they're finally gone," Octo-Cat said, standing with his forepaws on the low window frame as he watched the moving truck pull away. "They smelled bad, like human body odor. *Blech.*"

I rolled my eyes, but luckily he was too distracted to notice. "That's probably because they were moving heavy things for us the better part of the afternoon."

"Still gross. I have a very delicate olfactory operation up here," he said, twitching his nose demonstratively. Well, I couldn't really argue with him on that point.

"Are you good?" I asked, hoping he would go easy on me, though I half expected him to make me move his belongings from one place to another all night long until he came up with the winning arrangement.

"I'm good," he answered. His complacency gave me a wicked shock to the system. Would living here be like living with a different, less demanding cat? One could only hope.

"I'm ready for the funeral when you are," he

said, plopping his butt on the worn oriental rug and staring up at me with large, probing eyes.

The teacup—right. "Okay, I'll go get the box," I said, trying to remember if I'd left it in the car or tucked it away somewhere in the kitchen.

Octo-Cat raced ahead and blocked my path. "I said when you're ready."

"I am ready. We can do it now." *Aww,* he was being so sweet to consider my needs for a change. Maybe the loss of his teacup made him value the friends he had left. Maybe we really had reached a turning point in our relationship.

He shook his head and took on a condescending tone. "No, Angela. You are *not.* I wasn't going to say anything, because I assumed you already knew, but…" He paused to take a deep, dramatic breath. "You smell like human body odor, too."

…Or maybe nothing had changed at all.

I threw a hand on each hip and stared down at him. "So what? You want me to take a shower first?"

"Not want," he corrected, studying his paw nonchalantly. "Require."

I so badly wanted to call this whole ridiculous teacup funeral off, but instead I turned on my heel and headed toward the bathroom. Man, he really did have me trained.

As much as it irritated me to be told what to do by my cat, the hot water did soothe my aching muscles, and I felt more like myself after slipping into my favorite jeans and rejoining Octo-Cat downstairs.

"Ready!" I trilled, going once more to retrieve the teacup.

His furry form appeared at the top of the stairs, giving me quite the fright in the process. "No," he said simply. "This will not do."

"What's wrong now?" I asked, tapping my foot impatiently. That was one bit of body language he understood well since he often did the same thing by flicking his tail.

"Isn't it customary for humans to wear black when attending a funeral?" He tilted his head to the side as if it pained him to have to explain such a simple concept to me. After all, I was supposed to be the human expert around here.

"Yeah, but—"

He held up a paw to silence me. "That's what I thought. So, chop chop, you."

I sighed but went to find the dress I had worn to Ethel's funeral a few months back, anyway. At this point my annoyance was such that my cat was lucky we weren't headed to *his* funeral.

He's grieving. He's grieving, I reminded myself over and over again. But the truth was, he could be having the best day of his life and would still treat me this way. Most people had a sense of cats' haughtiness and entitlement but didn't know how deep it ran due to their inability to hold a conversation with their beloved animal overlords the way I could. Still, no matter how much he complained, Octo-Cat did forgive me for most of my flaws, so I did my best to put up with his.

The next time I came back down those stairs, I clung tightly to the handrail in case the tabby's agitation matched my own.

Octo-Cat gave me a purr of approval as he took in my black maxi dress and swept back hair. "Finally. Now come," he trotted through his electronic cat door and waited on the porch for me to join him. Once outside, I grabbed the tiny makeshift coffin—which had once been the box for a pair of flipflops I'd purchased from the discount shoe store—from my car's glove box and followed him to the side of the house.

He stopped at the end of a retaining wall that had beautiful pink azaleas spilling over the sides.

"I chose this spot," the cat informed me, "because these remind me of the pretty little flowers that once lined our dearly departed teacup."

When I squinted at the flowers and then down at the remains of the Lennox dishware in my hands, I realized that he was absolutely right. It was really quite sweet that he'd put so much thought into this. I wondered if he'd be so discerning when planning my farewell, should he outlive me. A morbid thought, it was true, but with all the murders around here lately, it was also a valid one.

"Should I go get a shovel?" I asked when he made no move to dig into the soft earth.

"That would be for the best, Angela." He bowed his head reverently. Was he praying? If so, what deity did cats pray to? Did he have the same God as me? And how did one send off a soulless object to the great beyond? So many questions when, honestly, I'd always just assumed my cat worshiped himself and expected me to join his strange religion as well.

I left him to his... *whatever he was doing.* There would be time for questions later. Now I had to respect the strange ritual I didn't quite understand but knew enough to see it was of vital importance to him.

Luckily, it didn't take me long to find a small hand shovel among the supplies in Ethel's gardening shed. As I jogged back to the scene of our interment, I wondered if Ethel had ever tended to the landscaping herself or if she'd always hired it out. I also wondered how long it would take for me to learn the specific care for each of the many types of plants that lined the property. Hopefully not so long that I killed some of them in my ineptitude. I really didn't want to have any more funerals for inanimate objects. Sure, plants were technically living, but I still didn't think they deserved to have funerals in their honor. Obviously, the teacup was a special case; I hoped this was obvious to my cat as well.

Returning to him, I settled onto my knees and began to dig in the spot Octo-Cat had pointed out. While I did this, he stood by and started a lengthy eulogy about the life and times of his friend teacup.

"It always gave me water when I was thirsty," he moaned. I decided not to point out that this was because he refused to drink from any other vessel.

"And unlike it's brother," Octo-Cat continued. "It was never contaminated by letting a fly into my Evian." His voice quivered as he continued, "No, sirree. It kept the water in and the flies out, just like a good teacup should do. I'll miss you, teacup. Breakfast just won't be the same without you. Nor will my dinner."

I worked very hard to keep my face straight, and thank goodness for that, because he turned toward me in complete seriousness and said, "Now it's your turn to say a few words."

Well, shoot. Why hadn't I prepared anything? I should've seen this coming from miles away. Still at a loss, I said the first thing that came to mind, hoping it would please him. "It was a good teacup. Pretty. Matched the others in its set."

"It did! It did!" Octo-Cat cried, and when he drew quiet again, I heard the unmistakable sound of a crash on the other side of the woods.

"What was that?" I whispered to my tabby.

He stood quietly, staring down into the open grave I'd dug for the teacup and its coffin.

"Did you hear that crash?" I asked again, more frantically this time. What if the murderer was back? What if he was coming for us and we were just sitting right out in the open, unmoving, not even looking?

My palms began to sweat. Thank goodness I was no longer holding onto the teacup, because I'd have dropped it to a second death.

Octo-Cat kept his eyes cast downward, still serious, still reverent, completely unmoved by my fear. "I think we're just about done here," he said sorrowfully. "Angela, will you please shovel in the dirt?"

I nodded and carefully pushed the dirt around the shoe box as Octo-Cat sang a mournful song with no words, only mews. It would have been beautiful, if I wasn't worried that it was leading a killer straight to us. Luckily, he closed his eyes as he sang, which enabled me to glance over my shoulder and keep an eye on the woods.

It took about five minutes to finish his wordless song. Our weird ritual now finished to his apparent satisfaction, he bowed his head one more time and said, "Okay, time to go play detective," then ran head-long into the woods.

CHAPTER EIGHT

I could scarcely keep up as Octo-Cat tore his way through the dense forest. Branches slapped into my chest as I wove my way deeper and deeper. The woods that joined the two properties didn't run more than fifty feet wide at the most, but with no clear path to guide me through, they felt much deeper and darker than they had by the light of the afternoon.

Even treading carefully, I managed to snag my foot on a knotted root, which sent me careening face forward into the dirt. Of course, I'd needlessly been wearing open-toed dress shoes for the teacup funeral, which made for a particularly painful toe-stubbing experience.

I moaned and rolled over onto my side,

clutching my poor injured toes and I searched the darkness for Octo-Cat. He'd probably made it all the way to Harlow manor by now, which meant I was alone in the creepy forest, sporting an injury that would make it difficult to escape quickly should trouble come calling.

An ominous crunch sounded a few yards away as something took slow, deliberate steps toward me over the bed of dried leaves that clung to the forest floor like a thick carpet.

Please don't be a wolf. Please don't be a wolf, I begged inwardly. Would wolves be brave enough to come so near a residential area? I had no idea, but the forest that linked our houses stretched far and long throughout the posh neighborhood. It was totally possible that some bigger animals had made their homes nearby and had now spotted me as an easy post-supper snack.

"Hello?" I called into the darkness, because it felt more terrifying to remain silent. Perhaps Officer Bouchard was still standing guard at Harlow Manor and would come running into the forest to rescue me. Hopefully he'd be at least a touch more careful than I had been.

The crunching leaves silenced, leaving me alone with the eerie howl of the wind sweeping through the trees. Well, I was never ever coming out here at night again. Nope, wouldn't do it, no matter how curious something made me.

And tonight seemed like a really good time to start my "no woods at night" rule, just as soon as I could get out of here.

I shifted onto my back and pulled myself to a seated position. Everything hurt, and I'd definitely be needing another shower. Thankfully, nothing appeared to be broken, so I pressed my already dirty hands deeper into the dirt and pushed myself to a standing position. My injured side had a hard time taking the weight, so I hobbled like a zombie, moving very slowly through the growth.

I'd only made it a few feet when the crunching started up again.

I wanted to run but knew attempting to move faster with my injury would only lead to another wipeout. So, I plodded slowly along with some unknown animal following in close pursuit. I'd reached the halfway point between the senator's house and mine when I heard Octo-Cat shout, "Oh, if you're looking for trouble, you've found it, all right!"

"Octo-Cat?" I called, turning behind me to search the trees for his tiny striped body. I'd never been so happy to hear his demanding, little voice in all my life.

Unfortunately, it wasn't him I found standing before me now. Rather, twin pairs of yellow-green eyes blinked into view, moving closer and closer until we were only a few feet away from each other. The white spots on the smaller cat made him easier to pick out, but the large black Sphynx remained mostly shrouded in the shadows, save for those large, glowing eyes.

Octo-Cat broke through the tangled limbs of the forest a few seconds later and looked me up and down. "What happened to you?"

"I fell," I said flatly, unwilling to take my eyes off our two strange visitors. Although, I supposed these woods belonged to them as much as it did us.

"Did they trip you?" He put himself between me and the other cats and growled, making me feel slightly safer and a lot more loved.

"I don't think so," I said, searching the forest floor for the nasty root that had caused my fall but coming up short in the expanding darkness.

"Well, I wouldn't put it past them," he mumbled.

The larger Sphynx stepped forward and let out a string of deep meows.

"Oh, jeez, not this again," my cat hissed in response.

"What did he say?" I asked, hobbling over to the nearest tree and extending a hand to rest on its trunk so that I wouldn't be stuck standing on one foot for this entire exchange.

As much as he'd hated working with the traumatized Yorkie on our last case, he seemed even angrier about having to speak to the Sphynxes. Octo-Cat took a deep breath before translating. "He said, '*at night the owl sounds in such a way our curiosity compounds.*'"

Well, that hadn't been what I expected. "Um, what?" I asked, shifting my weight to give even more of it to the tree.

"Not what," Octo-Cat corrected with a heavy sigh. "*Who?*"

"Huh?" I brought my free hand up to scratch at my head, completely baffled now.

He sighed again. "Remember how I told you I don't like their kind? *This* is why. It's not because they look funny. It's because they talk funny. Everything they say comes out as a riddle. It's why they're called Sphynx cats. Get it now?"

"You mean like the mythical creature that guarded the secrets of the gods?" I found it both crazy and fascinating that an old story I barely remembered actually had bearing on our modern world.

"Oh, it wasn't as selfless as that," Octo-Cat spoke as if he'd personally known the Sphinx of ancient Greek mythology. "It was a nasty demon, tormenting everyone just because it could." He spat toward our two hairless visitors and raised the hairs on his back menacingly.

"Wow," I said, hardly above a whisper.

Octo-Cat turned back toward me, somehow even more agitated than before. "So now you can see why I wasn't too keen to go chatting these guys up. The big one is Jillianne, by the way, and the little one is Jacques."

"I know you're a little uncomfortable right now," I said placatingly. It didn't escape me that each of the three cats had four good, strong legs, and I only had one. Despite his frustration, at least Octo-Cat had stayed by my side. "But we could really use their help," I continued. "Could you please just tell them that I'm their new neighbor and that I'm thrilled to meet them?"

"You know the ancient Sphinx enjoyed killing

people, too?" Octo-Cat licked his paw while talking, perhaps because he didn't like sitting in the dirty forest, or perhaps to show off that he had fur while our two conversants did not.

After a little back and forth, he informed me, "They say, and I quote, *'Whether written on note or banner or mat, this is our greeting, to human from cat.'*"

"Ha, they're saying welcome!" I cried, having far more fun now than my poor, long-suffering cat. "How do they come up with those so fast? They must be geniuses."

Octo-Cat growled. Once again, it seemed, our definitions differed. "I don't have to sit here and take this, you know. If you want my help, you'll refrain from encouraging their unwieldy behavior."

I thought he'd said they always talked like this, but correcting him now would just send him scampering off toward home, and I still had so much more I needed to find out from our two hairless wonders. "Can you ask them if they know who killed their owner, please?" I said instead.

Octo-Cat kept his eyes firmly on mine, a challenge. "This is getting old real fast, so I suggest you think over each question carefully, because I am definitely not doing this all night," he warned.

"Fine, fine," I groused. "Now, tell me, what did they say?"

He pressed his ears back against his skull and shook his head. "Yeah, you're enjoying this way too much, but I'm telling you right now, we are *not* adopting them."

I was just about to yell at Octo-Cat again, when he delivered the next riddle in a bored monotone. *"What we say to confirm, even if it makes one squirm."*

"Yes!" I shouted gleefully. "That means yes, right? They know!" This case really could be open and shut, seeing as we had two key witnesses right here and more than happy to talk to us.

Octo-Cat let out a dreadful groan, then turned tail and disappeared between the tree branches.

"Hey, wait!" I cried, slowly attempting to follow after him. I hoped the Sphynxes would follow, too. I was dying to ask them the next question. It would be the only one we needed to find the murderer—oddly my question would be the same as the answer to their first riddle: *Who?* As in, who killed the senator? How was Octo-Cat not getting this?

"They know who killed the senator," I shouted

after him. "Now you just have to ask one more question and we'll have solved this one in record time!"

I couldn't see him anywhere. Had he really just run off and abandoned me? And here I was starting to think he cared. Well, two could play the punishment game, and I suspected I'd have a much easier time annoying him than he had bugging me.

"Oh, Octo-Cat!" I called in one last ditch attempt to lure him in with kindness. "Where are you?"

Nothing. Even the wind had stopped howling through the trees.

Well, this was just great. He'd run off and left me injured and alone in a scary forest. Unless...

I turned around to search for the Sphynxes behind me, but instead bumped into a large, barrel-shaped chest. A human chest.

I didn't even bother to look at his face as I twisted around and made an attempt to run. Hurt foot or not, I needed to get back to the relative safety of my house. Needed to get out of these twisted woods now. My very life might just depend on it.

I'd only made it a single step, when he

grabbed my arms and pulled me back into his chest.

"Hey, what are you—?" I yelled as I struggled to get away.

He brought one sweaty hand up and clamped it over my mouth before I could finish my cry for help.

Well, this was it. This was how I died—not on the stairs but lost in the woods just a couple dozen feet away from my new palatial home.

This was not turning out to be a very good moving day.

Not at all.

CHAPTER NINE

This was it. Fight or flight. Preferably both.

I'd been detained by a murderer before. I'd been pitched into the wharf and left for dead. I could survive this. Summoning all my strength, I bit down on the fleshy palm that covered my mouth.

Yes! That did it.

My attacker cried out in pain. He pulled away at once, clutching his injured hand. "Ouch, what'd you do that for?" his voice came out a bit high-pitched for a man—nasally, too.

"Hey, you're the one who attacked me!" I corrected, studying his red face and matching red flannel pajama pants. He was far less scary now that I got a good look at him, but it didn't change the fact that he could easily overpower me with his size and strength.

"Who are you?" I demanded. "What are you doing in my woods?" He didn't need to know I'd only just moved in that afternoon. In fact, I'd probably be safer if he didn't.

At least he had the decency to look properly chastised. Still clutching his wounded hand, he rushed in with an explanation. "I heard talking, so I came out to see what was going on, and then you ran straight into me."

I scoffed and crossed my arms over my chest. It must be nice to be a man, to be able to wander into the dark woods with no worries for your safety beyond the normal serial killer with a chainsaw type of thing. Then again, I often found myself charging into dangerous situations with little more than my temperamental tabby to back me up. I guess that meant I couldn't judge him too harshly. "That still doesn't tell me who you are."

"I'm Matt Harlow," he said, thrusting his uninjured hand toward me in greeting.

"I bit the first. Do you really want to trust me with the second?" I asked, widening my eyes in challenge just like my cat so often did to me. I wouldn't feel safe until we got out of the forest. I was at way too much of a disadvantage here in the dark unknown with a much larger man before me and an injury slowing me down.

Matt jolted back and offered up a nervous laugh. At least he was scared, too. "Good point," he said. "So you're okay, right?"

"I'm fine," I said, even as the throbbing in my toes intensified.

"That's all I needed to know." He lifted his arm in a swift wave, then turned back in the direction he came from. "Have a good night."

I stood watching him go until he ducked out of eyesight, then continued my journey back toward home. So that was Matt Harlow, the senator's next of kin. Had we met under different circumstances, I could have prodded him for information, see what he knew. As it was, though, I'd much prefer to wait for the light of day and a reliable cell signal before possibly accusing him of murder.

Okay, so he seemed like a nice enough guy—tall, chubby, not unlike a teddy bear, but that didn't change the fact that his inclination upon meeting me had been to grab hold of me and cover my mouth. That was way creepier than those hair-lacking, riddle-smacking cats would ever be.

"I'm home," I called when at last I trudged through the door. I'm not sure why I even bothered announcing myself when clearly my feline roommate wasn't too bothered about my safety.

Octo-Cat intelligently remained hidden. Otherwise, I definitely would have given him a stern talking to about abandoning me in the woods right when the Sphynxes were about to reveal something crucial to our case. Well, if he wanted to hide from me, he could go to bed without dinner for all I cared.

I stomped through the house just to make sure he knew how angry I was with him. On my third pass through the open floor plan of the lower level, I stopped off at the kitchen to plop a fresh serving of Fancy Feast into Octo-Cat's bowl. As much as I wanted to teach him a lesson, I also didn't want to have to deal with an entire night's worth of his yowling.

But I got my jab in anyway, because I served him his least favorite flavor—the chicken we had only because it was part of the multi-pack I got from our local warehouse club store. Normally I saved up several dozen, then dropped them off as a donation for the local animal shelter, but I figured it would be okay to use one for a very necessary revenge.

Not satisfied, I marched up the stairs to my tower bedroom and wedged the door shut behind me. The cable company would be coming by tomorrow to connect the Internet, so for now I had to depend on my phone's mobile connection to surf the web before bedtime. Although the pages loaded painfully slow due to our proximity to the woods, I wanted to do some quick research into the senator's recent activity to see if anything jumped out as a possible clue to her murder.

While I was at it, I looked up Matt Harlow, too. From what I could tell, he was just a normal middle-aged guy from the city who'd recently gotten divorced and worked a job in sales. Nothing jumped out at me as serial killerish, but it was possible he'd only killed once to date, provided that Lou's untimely demise could be pegged squarely on her son's shoulders.

Honestly, I was stumped here.

An impatient scratching sounded outside my door.

"Go away!" I called, not wanting to deal with my diva cat just then.

Octo-Cat murmured a few soft words to himself that I couldn't discern, although it sounded like he was having some sort of argument. "I'm sorry!" he called to me after a slight bit of hesitation.

I was so shocked I dropped my phone onto the bed beside me. I don't think I'd ever heard that particular combination of words cross his lips. *"You'll be sorry,"* sure, but never a genuine, heartfelt apology.

I smiled to myself, ready to milk this moment for all it was worth. Just like Octo-Cat, I had to get my victories somehow. "What was that?" I asked, pretending I hadn't heard.

Whether he was here to demand a better flavor of Fancy Feast or because he genuinely felt bad, I didn't know. At least it was something, though.

When his voice came out strained, I could tell this moment was punishment enough. "You know what I said. You're just—*aargh!* I'm sorry, all right? I'm sorry!"

I raced toward the door as if in slow motion. Honestly, the moment wasn't that different from all those times the heroine runs in slow motion through a field of bright flowers to reach her hero.

Yes, I loved my cat, and this moment was special to me, so don't judge.

Swinging the door open, I smiled down at him and said, "I forgive you."

"Great," he said with a sly smile. "By the way, there's some nice green puke waiting for you at the bottom of the stairs." He trotted away, swinging his hips triumphantly. Honestly, I couldn't even remember what the green puke punishment was about, but I had bigger fish to fry.

Leaving my door open in case he wanted to come back for some apology cuddles, I snuggled back on my bed and returned to my research on the late senator and her next of kin.

First I read all the news articles pertaining to her from this past month. That bored me out of my mind, so I shifted my focus to what I personally knew already.

With the notes app on my phone open and ready, I typed in everything I'd discovered so far:

S*erved four terms, likely to be reelected.*
Died by falling down the stairs.
Bottom stair smashed in.

Mom asked to investigate for the news.

Icky gut feeling at the crime scene.

Two Sphynx cats from breeder in France.

Officer Bouchard stood guard outside for the better part of the day.

Mr. Thompson came to visit and was turned away.

Next of kin is Matt Harlow. He ran into me in the woods and covered my mouth when I tried to scream.

There, that was everything so far, right? If I considered everyone mentioned in the list that meant my first round of suspects included Officer Bouchard, Matt Harlow, Mr. Thompson, my mom, and some cat breeder in France. And, oh yeah, also her two cats. I should have probably added any person who was rumored to be running for the senator's seat in the next mid-term election, too. We were still more than two years away, which made me think a political opponent was rather unlikely.

That led me back to another very important question: how did the senator know Mr. Thompson? Sure, I could just ask him the next time I showed up at the firm for work, but would he be willing to tell me the truth or just send me further astray?

I Googled for close to an hour, searching for any connection between Harlow and Thompson, but came up short. Since I was still off work for the remainder of the week, I decided to call in a favor from a friend.

"Hello?" Charles, the junior partner at our firm and my former crush, answered in a hushed whisper.

"Charles, I need a favor," I told him.

"I'm at the movies with Breanne. Just a sec." I heard some angry groans from his fellow movie goers, then a minute later his voice came back loud and strong. "In the lobby now. What's up?"

"The senator was murdered today," I told him in case he didn't already know.

But he did. Of course he did. "They haven't ruled out the fact it could have been an accident," he corrected.

"But *I* have," I said, and he knew better than to argue. "Anyway, interesting fact: Thompson showed up this afternoon and tried to gain entry to the house, but the cops turned him away."

"That's weird. Wait, how do you know that?"

"I live next door now. Remember?" I answered matter-of-factly.

"You just can't keep away from a good mystery, can you, Russo?" he said with a laugh, even though we were talking about a murder here. It made my heart melt for him a little all over again. Seeing as he was spoken for, though, I swallowed back that particular feeling and returned my focus to the facts before us.

"Can you look into Thompson for me?" I asked. "Find out how he knew the senator? Why he showed up today?"

"Will do," he said. "That all?"

"Yeah, get back to your date, lover boy." I hoped he couldn't detect the sarcasm in my voice. Whatever the case, he quickly ended the call, leaving me alone in my giant house once again— and possibly with a murderer next door.

Maybe I could convince Nan to move in early? Then I would have a temperamental cat and a feisty old lady to protect me, should trouble come calling.

CHAPTER TEN

Despite another couple hours spent researching the late senator's life, history, and political stances, I didn't feel any closer to solving her murder the next morning. Sure, it could have been a big inheritance grab as had been the case with Ethel Fulton's murder, but somehow I doubted it.

As frightening as I'd found him last night, her polite and pudgy Midwesterner son didn't strike me as a killer—just a bit socially inept. Still, I couldn't rule him out completely. Otherwise I'd be left primarily with the two cats and possibly my boss as suspects.

Hopefully Charles would be able to find out what I needed to know about Thompson by the end of the day. I'd been there for him when nobody else was willing to support his "unwinnable" double homicide case. Against all odds, we won that time, and I knew we could win again. There was no case attached, but we at least owed the world the truth about Lou Harlow's death.

After a quick breakfast of dry Cheerios, I pulled back my hair and threw on a bold retro sundress, then climbed into my car. I wanted to solve this thing as quick as possible —not just for the senator, not just for the world at large, but for myself, too. Sleep had not come easily last night, and I doubted it would again until I knew I was safe in my new home.

"Where do you think you're going?" Octo-Cat demanded, jumping on top of my hood and staring daggers at me straight through the windshield.

"Next door," I informed him. I wasn't risking those woods again, whether or not the sun was now shining brightly. "Now get off my car so I can start the engine."

"I'm coming, too," he said, then sprinted toward the forest. Not surprising in the least. He had his preferred method of travel, and I had mine.

I navigated down my long, twisting driveway, down a small stretch of road, and then back up Harlow manor's long, twisting driveway. Yeah, once my poor foot made a full recovery, it probably would be faster to traipse through the woods, but sometimes fast wasn't the most important part of getting somewhere.

Like when it came to solving a mystery.

I'd learned that my first time out of the gate. There I'd gone, galloping toward that finish line without even taking the proper time to prepare myself for the race. And it had nearly gotten me killed.

Come to think of it, I'd put myself in mortal danger as part of solving my second case, too. This time I'd be real glad if bringing Harlow's murderer to justice didn't involve any flirtations with death on my part. It would certainly make me feel more professional if I could solve a crime without endangering *anyone's* life in the process.

Maybe today would be my big day—an important turning point for Ms. Pet Whisperer P.I. I chuckled at the notion, but admittedly my Mom's nickname had started to grow on me.

When I pulled up to the Harlow estate, I was surprised to see no police cars or sports cars in sight. Instead, a rusty old truck sat parked just before the main entrance. The door hung wide open, but I couldn't see anyone inside—not even the esoteric cats that I knew for a fact still lived here.

"I'm here!" Octo-Cat's muffled cry broke through the woods. "And I come bearing gifts," he added as he appeared carrying a dead rodent in his mouth.

"Gross," I said, already accepting that tomorrow morning's cat puke would be extra disgusting.

"Is someone there?" a deep voice called from within the house.

I hung back near my car and waited for the speaker to emerge onto the porch. When he did, I squealed for joy and ran forward to throw my arms around him. "Brock! It's so good to see you out in the wild." I hoped he wasn't offended by my choice of words, but it felt better to not directly mention that the last couple of times I'd seen him he'd been in either court or prison.

"Angie, right?" he asked, returning my giant grin. "Thanks for helping with my case."

Oops. Of course, he didn't know me as well as I knew him. I'd spent the better part of an entire week obsessing over his case, whereas he'd only ever seen me for brief periods in the middle of what had to be the most stressful time of his life.

"Hey, any time," I said with a playful fist bump against his shoulder.

"Well, hopefully never again," Brock corrected with a laugh. "But I appreciate the sentiment."

He looked good. Real good. His long, dark hair had been cut into a shorter style with just enough length left to it that someone could run her fingers through it.

What? Me? *No.* My last crush had ended horribly—with him dating someone else. And here dear Brock could scarcely remember my name. I didn't need to go fantasizing about the romantic possibilities between us.

Then again, his smile came easy and genuine. I couldn't believe that vile red-headed realtor was his twin sister. Other than their shared last name, they had almost nothing in common. At least not that I could see.

Brock motioned for me to join him in the

house, then crouched back down in front of the stairs and returned to work.

Those pants. That shirt. His muscles. And the way he handled that hammer... *Gah.*

It seemed my crush on Charles Longfellow, III, was all but forgotten. Falsely accused or not, I wondered if Nan would approve of me dating an ex con. Heck, she'd probably find it even more exciting than I did.

No, no, no. Bad Angie! I didn't have time to date —or even to really think about dating—when there was a murderer on the loose.

"So they hired you to fix the stairs?" I asked, just so that I had something coherent to say.

His dark, sparkling eyes were so pretty as he turned to study me. "Sure did," he said. "And I'm grateful for it, too. Even though I was acquitted, a lot of people around here still feel weird about hiring me."

"Oh, I could think of a few things for you to do." I grew hypnotized by the swell of his muscles beneath his jeans once more. Wait, had I said that aloud?

"What's that?" he asked, turning to me and running a forearm across his head.

"Uhh," I stumbled here, honestly unable to

remember what I'd been thinking. Then it hit me. As handsome as I found the man standing before me, this wasn't about him. It was about my own personal kryptonite—coffee. Suddenly, I remembered that I hadn't had any caffeine before coming over. No wonder my brain was applesauce. I needed to be way more careful about that going forward.

Pinching the inside of my arm to reinvigorate my senses, I finally smiled and said, "I have some jobs around my new place if you have the time. I live right next door, actually."

He stood and glanced toward my house as if he could somehow see it through the solid stone walls of Harlow manor. "Yeah, I'd love that."

Octo-Cat appeared in the doorway with traces of fresh blood on his furry face, but the carcass of his mid-morning snack thankfully nowhere to be seen. "No wonder you don't have a boyfriend," he muttered as he set to grooming himself.

Oh my gosh, my game was so bad even my cat could tell. Not a great start to my day. Not at all.

Octo-Cat's rude arrival reminded me that I had come for a very specific reason, and that did not include flirting with the help. "Actually, I just stopped by to see Matt Harlow. Is he here?"

Brock fished through a container filled with nails until he found the ones he wanted. "Nope, he left almost as soon as I got here. Will reading," he explained, keeping his focus now on his work. "Want me to tell him you stopped by?"

"Sure, thanks." With nothing else to do here, I turned back toward the door, shooting Octo-Cat a dirty look as I passed by him. He still claimed that all humans looked the same, but he had about a ninety percent success rate when it came to discerning a person's gender. I wondered if the Sphynxes had the same shortcomings he did. If they'd seen the killer but wouldn't be able to iden-tify him.

"Oh, wait. There was something I forgot," Brock called after me.

I turned around so fast, I practically spun in a full circle. My dress twirled around me like some kind of old-timey movie, and Brock chuckled.

"I just wanted to let you know that we have an official offer on your nan's house. Looks like your new roomie will be joining you in no time."

Oh, yeah. He and his sister were the ones in charge of selling Nan's house. The world did exist outside the two of us and my rude kitty commentator.

"Thanks," I told him. "That is good news."

I walked slowly back to my car, careful not to put too much weight on my injured foot. Now that Nan had a buyer for her house, she could join me much sooner than we'd originally anticipated.

I had zero shame in admitting that I was a scared little girl who needed her grandmother to tuck her in at night. At least until Glendale's newest murderer was caught and reprimanded. Maybe I could invite her over today to celebrate her pending sale and beg her to stay the night.

When she found out I had a mystery right next door, I knew she wouldn't be able to resist.

CHAPTER ELEVEN

Sure enough, Nan agreed to stop by later that afternoon to *get the goods* on our newest investigation—her words, not mine. Maybe I should have called my mom instead, seeing as she was already involved. But Nan had been a ready and willing partner the last time around and I liked her less direct approach when it came to questioning witnesses.

Had Mom not built a career for herself in journalism, I have no doubt that she could have made a fantastic prison guard. Nan, on the other hand, was an actress through and through. Even though her time on Broadway had ended almost fifty years ago, she still liked to don costumes and dive straight into whatever new character we needed to aid our investigations.

Me? I guess I was the brains behind our little operation. Whatever it was. Right now, we were still just impromptu vigilante detectives with a knack for finding both clues and trouble. Of course, if my mom had her way, I'd soon be hanging out my *Private Investigator for Hire* sign on the front lawn.

Nan was the actress, the good cop. Mom was the dogged reporter, ala bad cop, and I was the one who did all the research and then charged straight into battle without any regard to my own personal safety.

So maybe I wasn't really the brains, after all.

I unpacked some more boxes as I thought this over—as if any of it mattered, as if I were writing a novel or casting a TV show about our exploits. That would be the day! And it would be one both Mom and Nan loved. For now, I just wanted to get my clothes all hung and organized in my new closet.

I'd chosen the smallest bedroom in the entire manor not just because I loved the idea of living in a tower, but also because it felt more like home. Despite her flair for the dramatic, Nan had raised me to be humble and to find happiness right where I sat, and as such, the whole owning a mansion thing would definitely take some getting used to.

I let out a frustrated sigh when less than half of my wardrobe fit in the tiny tower closet. It may have been comprised mostly of thrift store and charity shop finds, but I loved every single article of clothing I owned and was loathe to part with any of it. They just didn't make clothes like they used to in the eighties and nineties. True, I'd hardly been alive during those decades, but it didn't mean that I couldn't adore the bold pops of color and fun patterns in the here and now.

"Who pooped in your litter box?" Octo-Cat asked, choosing that exact moment to creep out from underneath my bed. I hadn't even known he was there, the sneak.

"You have some really weird sayings," I told him with a frown before returning to the much bigger problem at hand. "And my clothes don't all fit in the closet."

"First of all, so do you." Octo-Cat sucked in a deep breath as he ventured into the closet to check things out. Coming back, he said, "And second, I really don't see why you humans need so many outfits, but you do realize we have six bedrooms in this house, right? Six! That's one more than the number of lives I have left, which seems more than enough to me. Just choose one of the other rooms and put your stuff in there."

I shook my head, wondering if I should ask more about how he'd lost his first four lives and what exactly that even meant. As far as I knew, I only had one life to live—only one to lose. That's why, even though our sleuthing was exciting, it could also prove to be very dangerous.

"C'mon," Octo-Cat said with a breathy exhale. "I think I know the perfect room for this, if you'll follow me."

I kept hold of the stack of hangers in my hands as I followed him down the spiral staircase and across the second floor of our new home. Well, new for me, at least. My cat had easily settled back in as master of this domain. I'd never seen him this at ease in my old rental, but then again, it seemed this particular tabby was born for greater things and more extravagant surroundings.

"This one," he said, stopping outside a closed door at the end of the hallway and pawing at the light streaming from beneath.

I opened it up and gasped, dropping my pile of hangers to the ground in a clattering mess. Somehow I'd forgotten about this room entirely. Sure, I'd toured the house a couple times before signing on the dotted line, but back then I was still enamored of the general luxuriousness that I had a hard time noticing the finer details.

And, oh, this room was fine.

First of all, it had a big window seat like the ones I'd coveted at Harlow Manor. The gorgeous piece of architecture stretched at least six feet long, which meant I could even nap there if I wanted. Heavy blackout curtains flanked it on either side. They must have been closed the other times I'd seen this place; that must have been why I didn't remember it. I liked that explanation much better than choosing to believe that I had either overlooked or forgotten such major details.

From the vaulted ceiling hung an antique crystal chandelier, which caught the sunlight and cast tiny rainbows all around the room. Most of the bulbs had burned out, but that didn't lessen its opulence one bit. The honey hardwood floors were scratched up but still sturdy. It wouldn't take too much work to sand them down and polish when I had the cash and the time—or maybe just the sexy local handyman—to do so.

"So, will this work as your new closet?" Octo-Cat said, hopping up into the window seat and taking a quick look outside before turning back to me. "It's small, so I figured you'd like it."

"Closet?" I gasped again. "No way! This is going to be my new library."

I'm pretty sure tears had formed in my eyes and were falling down my face and soaking my t-shirt, but I simply did not care. Octo-Cat could make fun of me all he wanted, but I'd finally found true, unreserved excitement when it came to our new digs.

How could I feel any other way, considering I now slept in a tower like Rapunzel and would have my own personal library like Belle? I'd stepped into a living fairytale. Sure, it turned into the Haunted Mansion ride when the lights went out, but… but…

Now I had my own personal library!

A loud rap sounded on the door downstairs, bringing our special moment to an end. Had it not, I could have stood there all day, sketching out plans for what the vacant room would one day soon become.

"Do we not have a doorbell?" I asked Octo-Cat, begrudgingly shutting the door behind me and heading toward the stairs to the first floor.

He shrugged and raced away to find out who had come calling.

As loathe as I was to step out of this beautiful daydream, I figured it might be Nan and she did not like to be kept waiting.

"Hello?" a nasal, masculine voice called.

A second series of knocks sounded, a bit more urgent this time.

Instantly, I recognized Matt Harlow as I spied his familiar shape through the stained-glass panes on either side of the front door. I flung the door open and stood blocking the inside. True, I had paid him a visit earlier that day, but I was still incredibly nervous around him—and nervous is exactly how I would remain until I could fully clear him as the killer.

"Hi," he said, tucking one hand in his pocket and using the other to offer me a friendly wave. I wondered if that was the same one I'd bitten the night before. "You stopped by earlier?"

I felt in my pocket to make sure I had my phone on me as an added security measure, then stepped back and gestured for him to come inside.

"Would you like to join me for some tea?" I asked, seeing as it was the neighborly thing to do.

Octo-Cat ran across the foyer, making terrible, ear-splitting noises. "Too soon! Too soon!" he cried.

"Is your cat all right?" Matt asked, craning his neck to get a better view.

I shrugged. "Eh, he'll be fine. Tea?"

"Sure, thank you." A genuine smile stretched right across Matt's face, and for the first time I saw the resemblance he bore to his late mother.

I led him to the formal living room and motioned for him to sit on the old Victorian couch trimmed in dark cherry wood. There were lots of different woods throughout the house, and I wasn't sure whether that was the result of poor planning or a decades-old decorating style I didn't quite understand. Halfway to the kitchen, I turned back, sensing I had the perfect opening to ask Matt a couple very important questions.

"You have cats, too. Right?" I hoped my eagerness to discuss the Sphynxes wasn't too obvious. Provided Matt wasn't the murderer, I would need him on my side.

He steepled his fingers before him. It seemed he was unsure of what to do with himself while he sat in my house. "Me? No, but my mom has always had them ever since I can remember."

"What's going to happen to the two that are there now?" I asked casually.

He shrugged and tried to get comfortable on the overly firm sofa. "I'm not sure," he admitted. "They've been hiding from me ever since I arrived. I thought maybe I could take them back home and give them to my kids, that way they'd be my ex-wife's problem instead of mine. But I worry those two might give my kids nightmares like the ones I had growing up."

"Nightmares? Why?" I asked, even though I already understood. Anything to keep him talking.

"Have you ever seen a hairless cat?" he asked with a shudder. "It looks like their brains are on the outside."

I laughed, and so did he. The description was pretty accurate. Even still, I'd begun to like Jacques and Jillianne now that I'd gotten the chance to talk with them a bit. Sure, they were a bit different, but they were also really stinking cool. "You mentioned having nightmares growing up. Have you always been afraid of cats?"

He cleared his throat and coughed into his fist. "I am not afraid of cats. I used to like them, but then Mom met that breeder in France and since then it's only been the finest purebred Sphynxes for her."

It seemed I had an opportunity here, one that seemed so fortuitous I hadn't thought it could ever happen. "If you wanted me to look after them while you decide what to do with them, I'd be more than happy to help out," I offered with an ingratiating smile.

"What?" Octo-Cat demanded, running back through the room and jumping up onto the couch beside Matt. "You can't be serious! There is no way I'll allow—"

"Sure," Matt said, interrupting my feline's tirade even though he didn't know it. "That would be great. That is, if you don't mind."

"Oh, I don't mind at all," I said with a huge smile, enjoying the expression of horror on my tabby's face.

"Traitor," Octo-Cat muttered under his breath.

Matt reached out to pet Octo-Cat but was summarily clawed by my very cranky kitty. "Ouch," he cried. "And that was my good hand, too."

The cat hissed and ran to hide in another room, shouting kitty curses at the top of his lungs.

"Sorry," I said, feeling a swell of embarrassment. I hoped he'd still trust me to watch his mother's cats after seeing how crazily the one under my care behaved.

"So, how about that tea?" I asked, scurrying away to the kitchen before he had a chance to refuse. This would give me a few private moments to plan my questions. If I asked the right ones, I just might find the missing pieces I needed to solve Lou Harlow's murder once and for all.

CHAPTER TWELVE

I brought Matt a cup of plain Earl Grey tea—
no cream, no sugar, no good, really. It would
have to do, though, seeing as I hadn't had time to
go to the store since moving in yesterday afternoon. Honestly, it was kind of a miracle that I
even had this.

"Thanks," he said with a friendly smile,
accepting the warm mug and holding it between
his hands. "Look, about last night, I just wanted
to apologize for… Well, I'm sure you remember."

"Water under the bridge." I waved off his
apology, even though I was happy it had been
given. I needed to keep him on my side if I were
to learn what he knew about his mom's murder.

"You're just being so hospitable and then

offering to take the cats, too. I feel really bad about how I acted. It's just…" He sighed heavily and turned the mug around in his hands so that the artwork faced me. It was my *crazy cat lady* mug. Nan had gotten it to celebrate my official adoption of Octo-Cat a few months back, and it had quickly become my favorite.

Matt sighed and cast his eyes toward the floor. "It may not be the manliest thing to admit, but I was terrified."

"It's understandable," I assured him. "After all, someone did just kill your mother."

"Exactly!" Matt lifted the tea to his lips, took a small sip, then set it on the coffee table. There weren't any coasters, but the old piece of furniture already had lots of wear, so I figured this wasn't a problem I needed to worry about at this precise moment. "I'm staying in her house, too. Granted, it was my house growing up, but it just gives me the creeps."

"My thoughts exactly." I reached forward to offer him a fist bump on the subject of staying in creepy houses. He didn't seem to know what to do with it, so we shook hands instead.

"So, you grew up around here?" I asked, taking a sip from my own mug. I couldn't stand tea without at least two spoonfuls of sugar mixed in, so I'd secretly filled mine with plain hot water. At least this way I could accompany Matt, make my questions seem more like a conversation than an interrogation.

"Not around here." He stopped and shook his head. "*Here.* Right next door."

"If you don't mind my asking, why did you leave?" I was really pleased with how things were going so far. Matt was opening up to me without even the slightest hesitation. How much more would he be willing to tell me before he reached the bottom of that tea cup?

"*Love.*" Matt snorted and rolled his eyes. "Lot of good that did me."

I winced sympathetically. Even though I'd never been in anything more than puppy love, I felt for the recent divorcee. Everything must have still been so fresh and new, and now he'd lost his mother on top of it all. "So, why don't you come back? I'm assuming your mother left the house to you."

"She did, but I don't know." He drummed his fingers on the side of his mug and frowned. "It would be hard to live there without constantly thinking of her."

"Was she a good mom?" I asked before taking a casual sip from my mug of hot water.

If Matt thought my questions were coming too fast and close together, he made no indication of it. Rather, he seemed happy to share, or at least happy to have someone to talk to. The poor guy.

"She was the best," he said with a nostalgic sigh. "Everything you read about her in the papers is true, by the way. She really had the kindest heart. Even before she got elected, she was always volunteering somewhere. In fact, we spent more of our Christmases serving up hot meals at the soup kitchen, then opening gifts at home."

"That's incredible. I'm sure a lot of people will miss her dearly. I know I will." I already knew this about her, of course, but hearing it from her son's lips made me that much angrier that someone had brought her life to an early and violent end.

Matt's eyes lit up with true warmth. "Did you know her well?"

I smiled. "Well, I voted for her every time I was able, and I could always tell she believed the things she said. It was refreshing."

Matt picked his tea up and took a long, slow sip. "I have no idea who would want to hurt her," he said, shaking his head. "It just doesn't make any sense."

"It could have been an accident," I pointed out, even though I didn't believe it myself.

"Maybe," he conceded.

We sat in silence for a few moments. He didn't say anything else, but I could also tell he wasn't ready to go, so I asked another question.

"When I stopped by earlier, you were at the will reading. Did everything go okay there?" I thought back to the first and only will reading I'd attended. It was the same one where I'd nearly died at the hands of an old coffee maker, where I'd discovered my powers and met Octo-Cat for the first time. As far as my experience told me, will readings could be a real riot.

"It was fine," Matt answered passively. "No real surprises. I got the house. My kids both got trusts set up for when they turn eighteen. Most of the rest of it went toward a scholarship fund she'd talked about setting up for years but had never got the chance to follow through on."

"A scholarship? That's nice," I said, nodding along. "For students who want to study politics?"

Matt scoffed. "No way. Mom always hated politicians. Even more so after she became one.

Said they were smart people with good intentions that got twisted along the way. But hers never did. God bless her soul."

"May I ask what the scholarship is for?" I asked, hoping it wasn't insensitive to track back after his tender words. "I mean, I'm thinking about going back to school, so maybe I'll apply for it." I wasn't really considering more school at the moment, but knowing me and my insatiable love of learning, it was really just a matter of time.

Matt glanced around my swanky manor house, his implication obvious—why would *you* need a scholarship? He didn't say that, though. Despite our rough start, I could tell he was kind, exactly the way his mama had raised him to be. "Biology. Or, more specifically, marine biology," he told me, and it was not the answer I'd expected.

Seeing the confusion on my face, he jumped in to explain. "I know, it seems weird for a senator, right? But back in the 70's, she'd just had me and my dad wanted her to stay at home to raise me. I guess that never suited her and she divorced him eventually, but before she did, she became involved with the new *Save the Whales* movement.

It gave her that first taste of political activism, and she was hooked."

He paused and took another sip of Earl Grey before continuing. "It's why she stayed in that big house by herself all these years. She didn't want to leave the ocean and all it meant to her. I guess I take after her a little bit myself because I made sure to get a place that overlooks Lake Michigan back in Chicago. Even now, I can't imagine looking out my window and seeing anything other than water."

"So, she wants to continue saving the whales through her scholarship fund," I summarized with a dreamy smile. "That's beautiful."

Another knock sounded at the front door, this one fast and light.

"Coming!" I yelled, jumping to my feet then squealing with happiness when I saw Nan through the stained glass.

"Okay, I'm here," she said as she stepped inside. She was wearing bright green galoshes and leggings patterned with rainbows. Up top, she wore an old T-shirt that had lost much of its original color from having gone through so many wash cycles. "Now catch me up on these riddle-speaking cats."

I turned toward Matt and made a funny face. "It's this book we're reading together," I explained quickly. Books really made the best excuses because few people would ask follow-up questions. It was sad but convenient nonetheless. "Anyway, this is my nan. Nan, this is Matt. Senator Harlow was his mother."

"Oh, you poor dear," Nan said, rushing over to sit beside him and pressing the back of her hand against his forehead. "How are you feeling?"

"Fine," Matt answered, though it sounded more like a question.

"I voted for your dear mama each and every time," Nan announced proudly. "They didn't come any better than her."

Matt raised his mug. "I'll drink to that."

I returned to my spot in the wingback chair across from them. "Matt was just telling me a bit more about his mom's legacy. Also, I've volunteered to watch the senator's cats while Matt gets the rest of the estate sorted out."

"One can never have too many opinions or too many cats," Nan said with a nod and a chuckle. Neither of these seemed true to me, but I let it pass.

Matt took another long drink of tea, then set

his empty cup back on the coffee table. "I should probably be going," he said, rising to a stand. "Thank you again for the hospitality and the kind words about my mom."

Nan stood, too, and gave him a warm hug. She looked so tiny wrapped around his big, bear-like form. Even so, I could tell he appreciated the gesture.

After Nan let him go, I got up and followed Matt to the door. "Let me know when you want me to come by for the cats," I said as we lingered at the doorway.

"Oh, right," he said in a way that suggested he'd already forgotten—or was pretending to have forgotten after Octo-Cat's little hissy fit from earlier. "Are you sure it isn't too much of an imposition?"

"I'm sure," I said, perhaps too quickly. The truth was I needed those cats. They held the key to busting this murder mystery wide open, and I really wanted to know what they would say. "In fact, maybe I should just come with you now? Give them some time to settle in before nightfall."

I couldn't risk him changing his mind, and now that I had Nan here, she could help keep Octo-Cat in a good enough mood to actually be useful. Even though I was supposedly his best friend, he clearly preferred her company to mine. I tried not to let that hurt my feelings.

Matt's brows pinched together as he studied me. "Are you sure you're sure?"

"The more, the merrier!" Nan said, slinging an arm around each of our waists and pulling us closer. "Now let's go get our guests."

Matt didn't say anything more as the three of us exited onto the porch. I searched around but didn't see any extra vehicles—other than Nan's souped up sports coupe—which meant Matt must have chosen to walk through the woods to pay me a visit.

And, even though he'd been a perfectly lovely companion for afternoon tea, this realization did not sit well with me. If he felt comfortable traipsing through the woods after our mutual scare last night, might he be willing to come through them again by the cloak of night?

Maybe I wasn't as safe as I'd hoped after all.

CHAPTER THIRTEEN

At the Harlow manor, Matt begged off to take a call, leaving Nana and I to locate and load up the two Sphynx cats. Despite our best efforts to be quick, it still took nearly an hour for us to find Jacques and Jillianne, catch them, and then get them back to my house. Apparently they were every bit as adept at hiding as they were at telling riddles. So that we wouldn't risk them slinking off again, Nan and I carried them straight up to the room I had dubbed my future library and closed the door tightly before letting them out of their carriers.

I'd also brought Octo-Cat in to join us, and I had the fresh scratches to prove how very *not* thrilled he was to be there.

"I object!" he cried, hurling himself at the closed door in protest.

"Oh, hush, or I'll give you something to object about." I had no idea what that might be, but luckily my mostly empty threat worked.

"C'mere, my sweet kitty!" Nan cooed, tapping her fingers on the hardwood floor where we both sat with our legs crossed.

Octo-Cat hated being called *kitty* but he loved Nan, so he traipsed over and climbed into her lap. She immediately fussed over him and began to scratch that special spot right beneath his chin. I could see the rage melt right out of him. Thank goodness.

"Let's make this quick," he said, eyeing me with obvious disappointment. Luckily I was used to his theatrics and his disappointment, so this didn't thwart my plans in the least.

The two Sphynx cats had retreated to the far corner of the room and sat shivering near the central cooling vent. They looked so miserable that I almost felt bad confining them here. Still, they had intel that we needed, and they were the ones who'd chosen to sit right beside the cold air pouring into the room.

The little one let out a croaky meow, and Octo-Cat sighed. Like he'd suggested, I'd do my best to make this as quick and painless as possible. If not for him, then at least for our two visitors.

"Let's go," Nan said, her eyes sparkling with excitement. "I can't wait to solve some riddles." I'd already told her everything she needed to know on the phone that morning, and now she was primed and ready to see some action.

"Okay." I focused my gaze on Octo-Cat, who did not return the eye contact. "Octo-Cat," I said again to get his attention. "If you want this to be quick, you have to pay attention."

He turned toward me with ears back and tail poofed. "Fine. What do you want me to ask the two hairless wonders?"

"Ask them who killed their owner," I said with the same impatient attitude I'd perfected as a teen.

Nan giggled gleefully, and Octo-Cat remained seated on her lap as he shouted toward the Sphynxes.

They remained in their dark corner, almost as if they'd been glued there. It took much longer for his back and forth with them than it had with our former terrier witness, and I'll admit I started to get a bit bored as the minutes passed by without any further answers.

Then, suddenly, Octo-Cat snapped his eyes toward mine, his whiskers twitched, and he did not look happy. "I knew it!" he cried. "You thought I was being breedist or whatever, but my first instincts were absolutely right."

"What do you mean?" I asked, rubbing my hands on my legs to awaken the sleepy nerve endings.

Nan glanced down at Octo-Cat with the dearest admiration as he revealed, *"They* killed the senator."

"Oh, c'mon!" I shouted. Was he really coming back to me with *this?*

He remained steadfast in his insistence of their guilt. "No, really. They just admitted it."

"Yeah? Then tell me what they said," I demanded, wishing I didn't have to rely on him to be my translator when there was a clear bias at play here.

"It would be a whole lot easier if you'd just take me at my word, you know? But fine." He sighed then recited back their latest riddle. *"'Ex-*

cuse us while we provide this breakthrough, for the guilt lies with the ones you see before you.'"

He was right, of course. The answer was obvious, but…

"That's not even really a riddle," I said glumly. "It's just a rhyme."

"Good gravy. They just gave you a confession, and it's pretty direct as far as their type goes. What more do you need?"

"Ask again in another way," I demanded, then whispered to Nan to fill her in while Octo-Cat talked with the Sphynxes some more.

Another several minutes passed before Octo-Cat addressed me again. "Well, Angela. They said, 'You didn't believe us the first time, but you already know who committed the crime.'"

Octo-Cat thumped his tail hard against Nan's leg, and she abruptly stopped petting him. "Good enough for you now?" he demanded with wide eyes.

"Not quite," I answered to his great dissatisfaction. "They say we already know, but I have a whole list of suspects. It could be Mr. Thompson or Matt or even Officer Bouchard."

"Or it could be the two freakazoids who literally just confessed to murder," he spat, shooting them a cold look, which he followed up with a hiss.

"What do you think, Nan?" I asked after relaying the latest clue.

"Phooey," she moaned, rubbing her temples in little circles. "I was never very good at riddles. Either of you could be right with your interpretations."

I chewed on my bottom lip while thinking about what to do next. "Okay, how about this?" I said, waiting for Octo-Cat's attention to snap back to me. "Ask them how they killed her. Not how she died, how *they* killed her."

"We already know that," he said, condescension dripping from each syllable.

I shook my fist at him and growled, which was enough to get him to cooperate for a little bit longer.

When he returned to me with their message, he stated it plainly with no commentary. "*Up it goes and at the same time down, it is here that the answer's found.*"

"Stairs," I said, recognizing a version of this riddle from my school days. "Okay, so that was *where*. I still need to know *how*."

He batted a paw in my direction. "You're insufferable. You know that?"

I could tell his patience hung on by a single frayed thread—mine did, too—but we weren't done yet. "Oh my gosh, please just ask them already!" I exploded. I'd wrongly assumed that his fondness for the senator would make him more cooperative this time around. Then again, this whole time he'd been certain that he'd already single-handedly solved the case. Who needed facts and testimonies when you have an ego the size of our entire home state?

Octo-Cat groaned and said, "You owe me. You owe me *so big* for this."

"Bigger than the mansion you requested after that last favor?" I shot back, refusing to be bested by a cat... again.

He rolled his eyes but revealed the Sphinxes' next riddle despite his protests. *"'Sure of foot and light of heart, this is how she fell apart.'"*

"Now I feel like they're just volleying my question back at me. This is going to take forever," I whined, resettling myself on the uncomfortable floor. I couldn't wait to fill this room with comfortable furniture and wall-to-wall shelves of books. I would have sat in the window seat for this exercise had Nan not settled on the floor first. Seeing as I was more than forty-five years younger than her, I shouldn't have been having this hard a time.

She reached forward and put her hand on my knee. "Honey dear, if you trust your cat, just let him do all the talking. It seems that might be easier for everyone involved."

If I trusted him. That was a huge *if.* Colossal.

Octo-Cat had clearly made up his mind before he'd heard even a single detail about Harlow's death. But still, I couldn't deny that the Sphynxes did seem to be confessing to the crime in their own special round-about way.

"You're right," I told Nan with a small smile, and then to Octo-Cat, "You don't need to translate for me. Just talk with them and then catch me up later."

He eyed me wearily, then hopped out of Nan's lap and joined our two hairless witnesses in the corner. After several minutes of mixed meows, he trotted back and took up his spot in Nan's lap once more.

"They did it. They killed her by tripping her when she was on the stairs. They are sorry and say they feel really bad about it. As much as I despise them, it doesn't seem like they did it on purpose, but who knows?"

"Thanks," I murmured. I felt a little better, seeing as he'd conceded one point. Earlier he had been certain that they murdered their own in cold blood. Now he was saying that they did it accidentally. Could this whole investigation really been all for naught? Were my instincts that wrong? I was supposed to be getting better with each case, not worse.

Just then, the phone in my pocket buzzed. I fished it out and read the new text message from Mom that popped up on my screen:

Police ruled H's death an accident. I'm coming over.

Well, that answered that.

I passed my phone to Nan so she could see the message, too.

"You don't really believe that, dear," she informed me, setting Octo-Cat to the side so she could push herself up from the floor in one smooth, fluid movement.

I struggled to a stand with far less grace. "I don't know what to believe any more," I admitted. The last couple days had passed in a dizzying whirl, from moving to snooping and everything in between. Both my mind and my body were exhausted. Was it possible I was seeing clues where none existed?

One look at Nan told me she hadn't given up on this yet.

And that was enough for me to keep going, too.

CHAPTER FOURTEEN

M om arrived about ten minutes later. That was the thing with small towns like Glendale—it never took long to get where you were going. I was a bit removed from the main village action, now that I lived on the swanky East side, but everything remained incredibly close and the traffic was generally light.

Nan pranced through the foyer to let her in, a fact which Mom did not seem happy about.

"Angie?" she asked, charging into the living room where she found me sitting with my smart phone. "What's she doing here?"

Not her politest moment, but my mom and Nan also preferred each other in small doses. Apparently personality types in my family skipped a generation, so if I ever had a daughter of my own, I'd find myself with a little girl who was both too garrulous and too ambitious for her own good. Nan and I had gotten the weirdo gene, and that suited me just fine.

"We were discussing the senator's death," I answered, hating the way the corners of my mother's mouth dipped even further.

"I thought we were working on the case together?" she said, her usual confidence strained. She glanced back toward the door as if debating whether she should make a run for it.

"We were," I said gently, hating that I'd hurt her feelings yet again. "I mean, we are, but..."

Nan breezed past Mom and plopped down onto the couch. "Oh, come off it now, Laura Jean. We're all in this together. Right?" She patted the seat beside her and motioned for Mom to join us.

"Right," I said, offering my mom a quick hug to lift her spirits. "Besides Nan hasn't been here long. Right?"

"Right," Nan answered with a wink that I doubt my mother missed. *Sigh.*

"Well," Mom said, shaking her head and tilting it to either side—a nervous tic she'd picked up during my toddler years, or so I'd heard. "As long as I'm still part of the club, I have some news to share."

She reached into her purse and pulled out a notepad. "First off, the death was ruled an accident. They think she may have had too much to drink at a charity fundraiser and then tripped and fell down the stairs."

Tripped over her cats, I thought, but didn't say anything. I still wasn't ready to talk to Octo-Cat in front of my mom and didn't want to invite questions that would require either doing so or telling her *no* when her feelings were already very clearly hurt.

"The next of kin came in last night," Mom continued. "Matthew Harlow, a divorced salesman from Chicago."

I nodded along mutely.

"The county has assigned a police detail to guard the place whenever he's not at home," Mom continued.

"A police detail. Why?" I remembered seeing Officer Bouchard there yesterday afternoon and how unsettling I'd found it. Nobody had been there this morning, though, when I stopped by. Well, except for Brock the handyman.

She set her notepad down and fixed her eyes on me. "Because the senator was such a prominent person in the area, they're worried that people might come by to loot or take souvenirs. It certainly doesn't help that she has one of the nicest homes in all of Glendale."

Mom widened her eyes at me. *And so do you,* her body language yelled loud and clear.

"So, what now?" I asked, that familiar sense of disappointment creeping up on me again. I should have been happy that the death was solved, but something still didn't feel right. "Case closed?"

"Ha!" Mom shouted. "Hardly! They can call it an accident all they want, but I know something fishy is going on here."

I grinned and gave Mom a high five. I was so glad we agreed on this vital point.

"And when the cops won't do their duty, it becomes the reporter's responsibility to find the truth. Right, dear?" Nan said with a placating smile.

"Right," Mom said, although she seemed less sure of herself now.

"I agree," I said, grabbing my phone and handing it to Mom. "These are my notes.

Granted, I have a few things to add after talking with Matt this afternoon."

"You met Matt? Without me?" Mom shook her head and kept her focus on the phone, but I could tell it really hurt her feelings.

"I'm sorry, Mom." And I meant it. I needed to try harder, now that the two of us had started spending more time together, now that we shared this interest. "It wasn't exactly planned."

"She ran into him in the forest last night," Nan said, leaning forward and clasping her hands together.

"*Nan,*" I cried. "Would you please just stop helping?"

I caught my mom up on all that she had missed in the past day and a half. "Sorry for not calling sooner. It's just been one thing after the next," I said when I'd finished.

"Thanks for filling me in," she said a bit too cordially for my liking. "But I should probably be off. Bye, Mom," she told Nan, who remained seated in her chair as I walked my mother to the door and said goodbye.

"Why do you do that?" I asked my grandmother when I returned. "You know it bugs her."

"That's why I do it," Nan said with a chuckle.

I placed both hands on my hips and stared down at her.

"What? She does the same thing to you!" Nan insisted, and she was right about that.

"Maybe let's all work a little harder on getting along." I fell back into my chair with a sigh. "I mean, we're all grown-ups here."

"As you wish."

"Great." Now, that Nan was properly chastised, this brought us to our next matter at hand. "So, will you please stay the night?"

A naughty expression crossed Nan's face as she laughed and asked. "To protect you from the monsters under your bed?"

I just glared at her, refusing to play these games. "You know why."

"I do," she said, nodding thoughtfully and appearing completely somber as she did. "I just had to get one last jab out of my system. I promise I'll play nice from now on."

"And you'll stay?" I asked, making no attempt to hide how important this was to me.

Nan nodded. "I'll stay."

I let out a giant sigh of relief just as Octo-Cat returned from wherever he'd been during my mother's visit. I assumed this was because he still hadn't forgiven her for the teacup incident yesterday.

"Um, hello there. Hi. What are we going to do about the two murderers you invited to live with us?" he demanded, nodding his head toward the upstairs.

"Oh, Jacques and Jillianne!" I cried. "I guess I should let them out of the library now. *Huh?*"

He took several steps back and squinted angrily, not unlike the expression I'd expect him to make if I ever dared punish him by spritzing him with a water bottle. That is something I would never in a million years do, though—especially now that I knew he could murder me with ease, should the inclination arise.

"Absolutely not," he said emphatically.

"But you said it was an accident," I reminded him, making slow work of rising to my poor, tired feet.

Octo-Cat flicked his tail so crazily that it looked like one of those giant, wavy armed blow up guys outside of an auto dealership. "Yeah, and do you want them accidentally killing you? You only have one life, right?"

"Okay, you have a point." I'd give him that.

As much as I felt for the two Sphynxes, I really didn't feel like dying today.

Nan watched with amusement as my cat and I talked, even though she only understood one side of the conversation. "If those two Sphynxes are staying in there, we should probably take them food and water. And a kitty box," she added.

"Good point." They were our guests. The least I could do was make them a bit more comfortable. "Octo-Cat, where did we put your spare litter box?"

"Oh, no. No way. No how. You have absolutely got to be kidding me. You give them my litter box, and I'll make extra sure I use your bed for all my kitty business going forward." Well, that wasn't what I wanted, but it also felt wholly unnecessary to need to head to the store to buy new supplies when we had everything we needed right here.

I sighed and asked a question I was almost certain I would regret. "What do you want me to do?"

"I want you to send them home. I don't like having them here." He remained tense, standing between me and the stairs.

"But don't you want to find out who killed the senator?" I asked, taking several steps closer.

"Uh, hello? We know who killed the senator."

I thought about this. Perhaps there was still a way I could get through to him. "Then shouldn't we keep them locked up until they can... um, stand trial?" I was reaching, I knew. I had no idea what animals normally did to mete out justice, but I knew Octo-Cat was a big fan of legal television shows. Hopefully appealing to his fondness for all things crime and punishment would convince him to start seeing things my way.

"Oh, Angela, you're absolutely right," he ground out, as if this possibility shocked him to the core. "I'll go stand guard."

"He's going to keep watch," I explained to Nan, wondering how I'd just managed to add kitty prison warden to my resume and if it would ever even come in handy.

Well, at least Octo-Cat was occupied.

For now.

CHAPTER FIFTEEN

I slept better with Nan staying the night. I still locked the door to my tower, but at least we were making progress in turning the giant manor house into a home. Soon my boxes would all be unpacked, Nan would officially move in with all the colorful old knick knacks that reminded me of growing up, and we'd hopefully catch Harlow's killer, too.

Lately, that was the stuff of dreams—or at least my deranged ones.

Feeling wonderfully rested, I awoke the next morning to the most glorious smell in all of human history.

Coffee!

Taking the stairs two at a time, I bolted

toward the kitchen. There, I found my dear, sweet, beautiful Nan standing with a polka-dotted apron tied around her teeny waist and a giant, steaming pot of coffee in her hand.

"Good morning," she trilled.

I'd have given her the hug to end all hugs if I wasn't worried that doing so might spill the coffee. In my huge rush to get everything moved in time, I hadn't even thought of what having Nan as my roommate would mean. So what if I was terrified of coffee makers after my near death experience? I still longed for that delicious, life-giving brew, and now, thanks to Nan, I would actually have it.

"Thank you, thank you, thank you," I cried as she grabbed my freshly washed *crazy cat lady* mug and poured me a cup. "Where'd we get the coffee maker, anyway?" I asked, after that first glorious sip of heaven on my tongue.

"I brought it with me," she explained, bending down to check on whatever she had in the oven. I hadn't initially smelled anything over the intoxicating aroma of the coffee, but now that I'd adjusted a bit, the scent of banana bread became unmistakable.

"You're still afraid of coffee makers, right?"

Nan turned back to me with a bright smile. She'd always been a morning person. Me, not so much.

I nodded anyway, too deliriously happy to be embarrassed as I took another gratifying sip.

"Well, then I guess I'll just have to be in charge of breakfast from here on out," she declared as she continued to move about the kitchen like she owned the place. I guess, in a way, she now did.

"Hey," I said after I'd consumed enough caffeine to perk up my brain. "Where did you sleep last night?" I'd had Ethel's old bedroom set hauled away, and Nan hadn't officially moved in yet, which meant her bedroom set wasn't here yet, either.

"I roomed with our two hairless visitors," she said her eyes aglow as she squeezed my bicep. "That window seat was so comfy."

"Nan," I scolded. "You're not supposed to sleep there."

She brushed off my concern by waving a dish towel in my direction. "I slept perfectly well, thank you."

"Regardless, I should probably call someone to at least get your bed moved here." I drained the rest of my coffee as I thought.

Seeing I'd finished, Nan immediately plucked the mug from my hands and topped it off.

"Oh, I could ask Brock," I realized as my brain continued to wake up. "He's already planning tp come by today to offer me some quotes on a few rennos around here. I'm sure he'd be happy to haul whatever you need over in that truck of his."

Suddenly, I remembered another thing we hadn't yet discussed. "When I ran into him yesterday, he said you had an offer on your house?"

Nan gloated at this news. "That's right. And I bet you'll never guess who."

Normally I didn't like guessing games, but I was still so happy from the coffee that I became a willing participant. "Mom and Dad?"

"Ha! Like they'd ever leave their place by the bay. Guess again." She wiped at the counter distractedly as she watched me try to puzzle out an answer.

"Is it somebody I went to school with?" I guessed. I couldn't think of anyone I knew in town who was looking for a new place, so I was completely stumped here.

Nan smiled and shook her head. "Nope, but it

is someone we both know. Someone who's quite handsome."

I leaned back against the counter, mug still in hand. *"Hmm."* Nan was a shameless flirt and found half our town handsome by my most recent tally. I knew her latest crush was on the much younger Officer Bouchard, but he didn't strike me as the type to appreciate a retro, cozy Cape Cod in a landlocked neighborhood.

Unable to control her excitement anymore, Nan burst out with her big reveal. "Why, it's our very own Charles!"

I laughed at her joke, but Nan just kept staring at me with that earnest look in her eyes. "Wait. You're serious?" I squeaked.

She bobbed her head enthusiastically and did a happy, little twirl. "Dead serious. He said it was time he put down some roots now that he'd made partner."

"Nan, that's wonderful!" I cried, dancing with her now. "Since we're all friends, you may even be able to visit your old house from time to time."

"Oh, I'm counting on it," she said, her eyes glinting with untold mischief as she transitioned into a fast foxtrot that I had no hopes of replicating. "A happy ending for everyone."

A gentle rap sounded on the front door, drawing both of our attention.

"I'll get it," I told Nan, placing a hand on her shoulder as she stilled her movements. "You stay with the banana bread. I want a piece as soon as it's out of the oven."

"Roger that," she said, offering me a salute for reasons I didn't understand. Then again, if I understood even half of Nan's schemes, I counted it a good day. So far we were off to a great start.

I padded toward the foyer with bare feet, messy bed head, and a half-full mug of coffee. When I spied who was on the other side of the stained-glass windows, my heart screeched to a stop. Okay, not really, but it may as well have, given the absolute shock and horror I felt in that moment.

Brock saw me before I was able to duck out of view and gave a friendly wave. There would be no retreating now. *Oh, poop.*

I turned my back and wiped the sleep from my eyes, then put on my best closed-mouth smile and opened the door. "Good morning."

"I hope it's not too early," he said, looking me up and down as he assessed my hot pink pajama pants and spaghetti string tank top.

"Nope, you're right on time. Come on in. Nan!" I called back toward the kitchen. "Brock's here and we're going upstairs."

"Okay, boss!" she shouted back.

Brock frowned and pressed his hand to the stair bannister, stopping in place. "Yeah, about that… Could you please not call me Brock anymore?"

This surprised me so much I forgot about my desire to keep my mouth closed until I'd had the chance to brush. "What? Why not? Isn't it your name?"

He sucked air through his teeth before saying, "It is, but that name is so associated with the trial now, I kind of cringe every time I hear it."

That definitely made sense. The man had been accused of a double homicide, and for months everyone in Glendale was convinced of his guilt. I didn't blame him for wanting some way to mark a fresh start.

"Oh, of course. What should I call you instead?" I asked with another closed-mouth smile.

He let out a giant sigh of relief. "How about Cal? Short for Calhoun, so it's still my name, but it's not tainted like the longer version."

"You've got it, Cal," I said, then made a dorky, little clicking noise and pointed my finger at him like a fake gun. Really not cool.

He seemed to find it endearing, though, because he laughed. "Thank you, Ang."

We headed upstairs to the room that served as both my future home library and the makeshift kitty prison. Octo-Cat stood stationed outside the door, appearing as if he hadn't slept a wink all night. That would be like eschewing sleep for several days, had he been human. I shuddered to think at just how cranky he would be until our Sphynx visitors were released—or at least transferred to another prison.

"Go get some sleep, you," I told him in a cutesy voice, the kind a normal cat owner might use when talking to a normal cat.

He yawned and stumbled off.

After entering carefully to make sure no Sphynxes escaped in the process, I turned to Brock and explained, "This is my favorite room in the whole house. I want to build shelves right onto the walls, spruce up the floors, add some more lighting, and turn it into a library. What do you think?"

"This is the perfect place for that," he said,

turning in a slow circle in the center of the room. "Hey, aren't those the senator's cats?" he asked upon spotting Jacques and Jillianne shivering in their favorite icy corner.

"It's a long story," I said, moving back toward the door. "Could you maybe grab some measurements for me real quick? I'll be back in five."

Once he agreed, I latched the door behind me and then raced to the bathroom to run a brush through my hair and a toothbrush through my mouth. I also splashed some cold water on my face, but decided doing anything more would probably be overkill.

"It shouldn't be too much for me to do the work you're looking for," Brock—oops, *Cal*—said when I returned. He'd been standing by the window seat that looked out onto the beautifully landscaped backyard. You could just barely see the ocean beyond the tips of the trees, and it was a lovely sight to behold.

"That's great," I said, joining him at the window and feeling a little shiver of excitement overtake me. Even with caffeine rushing through my system, I still found myself a bit tongue-tied with this gorgeous man so near. "How much, and when can you get started?"

Cal told me a figure that made me a little sick to my stomach until he explained that this would include the custom-built shelving I needed to line my walls. After that, it seemed like a steal. I couldn't believe that this prince would be building me my fantasy library.

Dreams really did come true.

We shook on it, and then he said, "It's early enough that I can actually get started today. Like I said, not a lot of folks are lining up to hire me, given my recent history."

"You've got yourself a deal, Cal Calhoun," I said with a huge smile, thrilled that we'd be spending more time together. Partially because he'd be nearby in case of danger, and partially because I most definitely had the hots for him now. "Nan and I will both be around unpacking some boxes today. Just holler if you need anything."

"Will do."

"Oh, and Cal?" I had to keep saying his new name to get used to it. The more I said it, the more I liked it. It was uncomplicated and appealing, just like the man himself.

"Yeah?" He removed the measuring tape he'd

brought with him and let its long yellow tongue snap back into place.

"Do mind the Sphynxes. They're slippery little buggers," I said, parroting the words Officer Bouchard had said to me just a couple days ago.

And with that, I slipped out of the room and ran up to my tower to find the perfect outfit for casually running into my new crush later that day.

CHAPTER SIXTEEN

My phone started ringing aggressively while I was mid-shampoo. I shut the water off, grabbed my towel, and jumped out just in time to catch Charles before his call got routed to voicemail for a second time.

"Hello?" I asked, dripping onto the cold tile floor. I pushed open the old window with a creak. At least that would let some warmth in here.

"Angie, it's me," Charles said as if he somehow didn't know that caller ID existed and was standard on all phones these days.

"What's up?" I asked, hugging my towel tighter around myself. Of course we'd be having this conversation while I was wet and naked.

Knowing my luck, I'd slip on one of the many puddles forming below me, hit my head, get knocked unconscious, and then Brock—I mean, Cal—would have to bust through the door to save me. Maybe I'd even wake up with a second secret super power while I was at it.

Okay, now I was wet, naked, and in a panic. I carefully lowered myself to sit on the edge of the tub while Charles explained the reason for his call. At least, if I fell from here, I'd have a shorter way to go before hitting the floor.

"Sorry I didn't call back yesterday." I heard the unmistakable sound of a door shutting on his end of the call. He paused before explaining further, "Thompson took a couple days off for bereavement."

"For the senator?" I asked, not expecting this news about my workaholic boss.

"Yup," he said, sounding every bit as surprised as I felt. "Apparently the two of them were closer than any of us knew."

I gasped, almost losing my balance and scrambling not to fall. "Were they having an affair?"

"Oh, c'mon," Charles ground out. "Thompson and Harlow, really?"

"Well, anything's possible," I mumbled defensively.

"That's not what was going on," he said with obvious irritation.

That didn't stop me from continuing my line of questioning. He had information, and I needed to know it sooner rather than later. "Then what was?" I demanded.

"Get this," Charles said, and I could just picture him smiling as he paced around his office. He so loved revealing shocking twists, the smoking gun. I wondered if that was what we had here now. "Harlow was planning on stepping down. She was grooming Thompson to run for election as her hand-picked successor."

"Thompson?" I exclaimed. "But he's awful with people." Not only did he insist on calling everyone by their last names, but he often openly criticized me and the other people at the firm. I knew it was all to protect our stellar reputation, but still. The thought of him as an elected politician representing my state made my stomach churn.

"Maybe," Charles said, apparently unwilling to badmouth the senior partner the way I was.

"But there's no denying he's smart and, believe it or not, he and Harlow share a lot of the same political views, too."

"Like what?" I cried, still unable to believe what he'd just revealed.

"They've been friends for a long time. In fact, they met more than thirty-five years ago when they were both doing grassroots work for the *Save the Whales* movement. Thompson said those were some of the best years of his life."

There was that *Save the Whales* thing again. Could it be important? Important enough to cost the good senator her life? And, if so, did that mean Thompson might be targeted next?

"Charles?" I said, knowing I could trust him with this. "Do you think the senator might have been murdered for something to do with her environmental activism?"

"Then or now?" he countered, and I could tell that big, beautiful brain of his was already thinking hard.

"Either," I said. "Is there anything you know that could give some insight into why somebody might have wanted her dead?"

He sighed. "You know the police ruled her death an accident."

"Yeah, but I doubt you buy that, either."

"It *is* suspicious." He thought for a moment before saying more. "How closely do you follow national politics?"

"Not very," I admitted. "I did some Googling on the senator and any recent pieces mentioning her, but nothing jumped out at me."

He chuckled. "Well, here's a quick recap. Last week it was announced that a major oil company had petitioned to put in an access pipeline. It's a new proposal, but people are worried about it. Most of it would run right through our state, even cutting off the corner of one of our national parks."

That sounded awful. I loved my home state for its natural beauty and proximity to the ocean just as much as the senator had. Some giant oil operation would take part of that away, and for what?

"I can see why the senator wouldn't have wanted that, given her deep love for the environment," I told Charles.

"It's still got a while before it goes to vote, but Big Oil is lobbying hard to make it a reality. Their argument is that it would create jobs and bring us another much-needed local energy source, thus lessening our dependence on foreign oil." He explained everything pedantically without a hint of how he felt about the proposal. Seeing as he was a recent transplant from California, I found myself wondering whether Charles sided with Big Oil or the national parks. I knew where I stood.

"But the senator wouldn't have been okay with the destruction of one of our national parks, I take it."

"She definitely wouldn't have been, though it's only about five-thousand acres and the pipeline proposal includes building a new protected park farther upstate." Was he playing devil's advocate for the sake of argument, or did he truly believe the pipeline was anything other than a disaster waiting to happen?

I grew frustrated and let out a massive groan. "What's the point of protecting it, though, if anyone with enough money can destroy it on a whim?"

"I see what you're saying, Angie. I do." Charles sighed and paused for a moment. "But you have to understand, our checks and balances are put in place for a reason, and they work, too. It's not a whim. If the pipeline is going to get approved, a majority of the senate needs to vote in its favor. And, as you know, Harlow was just one out of a hundred."

I ran my fingers over the soft edges of the towel. My skin was quickly moving toward dry as this conversation carried on, but my hair was still a shampoo-y mess. "So then why would the murderer single out Harlow?" I asked.

Charles's voice grew quieter, leading me to believe someone might be passing outside his door and that, for whatever his reasons, he wanted to keep this conversation private. "Let me once again remind you that we don't know whether there was any foul play involved, but if there was, then there'd be a lot of reasons one might single out Harlow."

Oh, this was getting good. Maybe Charles had the smoking gun after all. "Such as?" I asked, my curiosity reaching a fever pitch.

"For one, as one of the two senators repre-senting the state where the proposed pipeline would be built, her opinions hold a little more sway," he started, paused, then raised his voice back to its normal volume. "Add to that the fact she was a mostly conservative politician who could be pretty much guaranteed to vote with the Democrats on any issue that even touches the environment. With a split senate like we have, she could very well end up the deciding vote when the issue goes to vote. Or at least, she could have been."

A knock sounded on the other end of the line.

"Just a sec!" Charles shouted, then said to me, "I need to go."

"Thanks, Charles," I said. "This has been hugely helpful and given me lots to think about."

"Angie, wait." He paused. When he spoke again, his voice sounded lower and far more serious than before. "Please be careful. If you're right and there's some huge political conspiracy underfoot, then you could find yourself next on the hitman's list. Let it go. I'm begging you. Let the authorities deal with whatever did or didn't happen. Okay?"

"Okay," I said agreeably, crossing my fingers just in case. I didn't want to worry Charles, but at the same time, I was so close to having this thing solved it just didn't make sense to back out now. "Thanks for the call. Bye."

I hung up before he could offer any further

argument, finished my shower, got dressed, and went to find Nan.

With any luck, we'd have this case wrapped by nightfall.

And maybe for once, luck might actually be on my side.

CHAPTER SEVENTEEN

For the better part of that afternoon, I thought about all the locals who might benefit from that proposed pipeline. How much did one need to get out of the situation to consider murder a viable option?

I suppose someone unemployed could want a job bad enough to take such drastic measures, especially if he had a family to provide for. But the proposal was still very new, which meant the news hadn't stretched too far about what could be coming our way. Even though I didn't follow current events as much as I probably should, I still learned about most major stories via my various social media accounts.

This one hadn't made the rounds yet. At least not within my network.

Harlow's murderer had to be somebody on the inside. Someone who paid close attention to the news, or made it even.

Pondering this further, I put a call in to my mom. Unfortunately, it went straight to voicemail. *Boo.*

I spent some quiet time researching on my laptop but continually came up short. I'd talk to Nan about my conversation with Charles soon, but she had a hard time keeping quiet when she got excited. Her voice would echo like crazy through this giant house, and with Cal still here working in the library, our talk would just have to wait.

After another hour passed, I tried calling Mom again. She would never give up on a story before it reached its satisfying conclusion and, seeing as she was the one who reported the news, she most definitely would know more about the pipeline and even its possible benefi-ciaries.

Still no luck. *Grr.* She must have her phone turned off, which was almost never the case with her. Maybe she and Dad had decided to catch a matinee at the new movie theater the next town over.

Agitated and unable to sit and wait any longer, I decided to go see how things were going in the library. Maybe I could find a nice way to send Cal home early so that I could talk my recent finding over with Nan.

"Knock, knock," I called before pushing my way inside.

The room had grown chilly, and I wrapped my arms around myself as I stepped into the library. Glendale had reached that special time of year where the days were sunny and warm, but both morning and evening temperatures dipped uncomfortably low. The library's large bay window hung open, its sheer drapery fluttering inward.

Cal wasn't there, and neither were the two Sphynxes.

Oh no. This was not good at all.

I raced down the stairs, searching for somebody, anybody.

Cal stood outside, loading up his truck. "I'll be back tomorrow if that's okay," he said before taking in my panicked expression. "Uh, is that not okay?"

"Did you leave the window open up there?" I demanded. My voice came out crazed and shrill, which I hated. "The cats are gone."

He pushed the door on his truck bed up and gave me a pained look. "Shoot. I'm sorry. Let me help you find them."

Not able to wait any longer, I raced around the perimeter of my yard, hoping to find our two missing house guests while Cal searched closer to the house. He must have informed Nan at some point, because she came outside to help, too.

"I didn't leave the window open," he said when our paths crossed again. "I did open it briefly to air out some of the dust, but I kept my eyes on the cats the whole time. When I shut it again, they were still in the room."

"I believe you," I said, but that didn't lessen my worry any. What would Matt say when he found out the cats I'd begged to babysit were now runaways? Whether or not he wanted to keep them, he most definitely would not be pleased that I'd managed to lose one of the last reminders of his mother.

I peered into the forest uneasily. Would I have to brave those woods again? Would Octo-Cat be willing to help? And just where was he anyway?

I spotted a little red sports car in front of the Harlow place. It seemed Thompson was over for a visit with Matt. Hopefully that would keep him occupied long enough for me to safely recover the missing cats. We looked for another half hour, but by that time, dusk had begun to settle in.

"I'm really sorry again," Cal said when we still hadn't made any progress. "Is it still okay for me to come back tomorrow?"

"Of course. And seriously, don't worry about it. I know this wasn't your fault," I assured him.

He nodded grimly, then ambled over to his truck and sputtered off.

"I'm going to go start on supper," Nan announced, giving me a sympathetic pat on the shoulder. "Don't worry, dear. I'm sure they'll show up soon."

I worried my lip while taking another loop around the property. Why were these Sphynxes so good at hiding? And why wasn't Octo-Cat here to help?

Giving up at last, I trudged up the stairs and went to investigate the upper floors of the house. Maybe they hadn't gotten outside at all. It was possible they were just tucked into some other cold corner, shivering with abandon. Seriously, what was up with their desire to be cold all the time?

The house itself had dropped a few degrees since my last pass through. Much to my chagrin, I found that I'd left the bathroom window wide open following my chat with Charles. I eased it shut again, finally deciding I'd earned a break. I could search again later with fresh eyes. First, I just needed to sit a while.

As I approached the stairs, a shadow shifted at the end of the hallway. I squinted for a closer look, wondering if at last I'd found the Sphynxes, and just as I was about to give up the search, too. Unfortunately, it wasn't the cats—just my poor, overworked imagination. Keeping my eyes on the beautiful stained-glass windows in the foyer below, I stepped down and directly onto Octo-Cat, who hadn't been there even a second earlier when I'd glanced down to ensure I had a clear path.

He let out a terrible, twisted yowl, and I quickly adjusted my weight to avoid hurting him any further. This adjustment caused me to lose my balance and tumble down several steps before catching myself halfway down.

"You tried to kill me!" I shouted, clutching my

throbbing head. I'd hit it—I'd hit *everything*—on the way down. "You really tried to kill me!"

Octo-Cat widened his eyes in horror. "It was an accident," he insisted, hobbling down for a closer look. I could tell he was hurting, too, but he'd live.

Me? I'd almost been murdered by my cat, and I had no idea why.

Nan came rushing in. "Angie, goodness! Is everything all right?"

"Octo-Cat tried to kill me," I screamed again. How could this be real?

"No, Angela, no!" he continued, not even flicking his tail or making any of his usual irritated gestures. "It was an accident. There was a shiny red dot. I didn't mean to—"

Suddenly, the front door burst open. My mom stood there, backlit by the setting sun, her hair wild with twigs sticking out of it at odd angles. "Get in the car now!" she told me. "Mom, your keys!" she told Nan.

"I didn't do it! I didn't do it!" Octo-Cat cried, but I could deal with him later. I ran down the steps as fast as I could and hopped in the passenger's side seat of Nan's sexy red sports coupe.

"What's happening?" I cried as Mom joined me and jammed the keys in the ignition.

The engine roared to life and she pushed the car into high gear, creating a giant cloud of dust behind us. We took off so fast, the momentum whipped me back against the seat hard. My head began to throb again, but the physical pain was nothing next to the morbid curiosity I had for whatever came next.

"Mom!" I shouted, holding on tight to the dashboard as we flew down my driveway and turned onto the road ahead. "What is happening?"

"I saw who tried to kill you," she said, and for the first time I noticed she was panting with exhaustion. "I was in the woods and came running the second I saw him slip out of your window. He killed Harlow, and now he was trying to kill you. My little girl! If I catch him before the cops do, he's dead."

"Mom!" I screamed again just to ensure I could be heard over the roar of the engine. She made another sharp turn, and Nan's hot little ride fishtailed onto the main road that ran through Glendale. "Who? Who tried to kill me?"

She gripped the steering wheel so tight her

knuckles turned white, but she only gunned the gas pedal even harder. We crossed the train tracks, and Mom practically lost control of the vehicle. Still, we were moving forward at speeds faster than any car should even be able to drive.

"C'mon, c'mon," she muttered, her jaw set in a determined line.

Sirens wailed behind us, and I recognized one of the county patrol cars as it pulled up behind us and quickly gained speed.

"Mom!" I cried. I still didn't know what was happening, but it felt like I'd been saved by one murder plot only to wind up right in another one. "Stop! The police are behind us!"

"Good," she said, taking another deep breath as she accelerated even faster. The speedometer edged dangerously close to the one-hundred and sixty miles per hour mark. How was this possible? Why were we even doing this?

Panic gripped me hard as we continued our wild ride. Oh my gosh, someone had tried to kill me, and now I was going to die at the hands of my mother's crazy driving!

"Where would he go?" Mom shouted at me. "Where would he go next?"

"Who?" I screamed again. I still didn't understand anything.

"Your boss," she ground out, changing lanes with abandon. "Richard Thompson."

CHAPTER EIGHTEEN

My mind reeled while my body slammed against the car door and my seatbelt dug into my chest. Did my mom really think that my boss had tried to kill me? That couldn't be possible. Octo-Cat had tripped me. I'd never even seen Thompson that day.

"Mom," I said, hyperventilating. "I'm not sure what you saw, but Thompson was never at my house."

"Yes, he was," she shouted, taking another sharp turn.

We were going toward the law firm, I realized then. The cop car stayed right on our tail. I turned back and saw Officer Raines's determined face as she pursued us. She and Mom had already gotten off on the wrong foot, and this impromptu high-speed chase pretty much ensured they'd never be on friendly terms, no matter what happened next.

"I don't know how he got in," Mom continued. "But he climbed out through the window."

"When?" I pleaded, still not understanding. How could any of this be real?

"About two minutes before I made it to your door," she said, slowing slightly as we passed by the law firm. Thompson's car was not there.

That timing Mom reported lined up pretty well with my fall, but...

"There weren't any cars. I didn't see or hear anyone leave before us," I insisted. Even if Thompson had somehow managed to get in and out of my house without being detected, he hadn't gone anywhere in that little red sports car of his. The irony didn't escape me that the pursuant and the pursuer had the exact same type of vehicle. What a chase this would have been, had Thompson actually been a part of it.

"Of course," Mom yelled, twisting the car in an action movie-like U-turn. "He's still on foot! We have to get back! Your nan!"

Fear gripped every fiber of my being as I

thought of my poor, vulnerable grandmother all alone with a killer. She was tough, but that was all attitude. If he came at her physically, she wouldn't stand a chance.

The sirens whooped behind us. "Pull your vehicle to the side of the road," Officer Raines commanded over the loud speaker.

"C'mon, Mom," I said, still clutching tight to the dashboard. "Get us back to Nan!"

I had no idea where my mom had acquired her wicked stunt driving skills, but she got us back to the manor house in record time, which was saying a lot considering how quickly we'd initially peeled away.

As soon as the scar skidded to a stop, I jumped out and raced toward the house, stumbling on the porch stairs as I went. "Nan!" I cried. "Please be okay!"

Nan appeared in the open doorway wearing her polka-dotted apron and drying her hands on a dish towel. "Of course I'm all right, dear. Just finishing up dinner. Did you and your mother have fun on that high-speed chase of yours?"

I hugged her tight but was quickly pulled back by one very angry Officer Raines. Somehow, she already had Mom cuffed and face down in the dirt. "Stop!" I screamed. "We aren't the bad guys!"

Officer Raines slapped a pair of cuffs on me anyway and began to cite my Miranda Rights.

Mom struggled on the ground. "He's still here somewhere. He tried to kill my daughter!"

The lady cop did not seem amused. "Likely story," she mumbled.

But Nan poked her hard on the shoulder, causing us all to gasp. "You listen here, missy! If my daughter says there's a killer on the loose, then you better believe there's a killer loose. So what if she went a little over the speed limit? Is that as bad as having a murderer on the loose?"

Officer Raines laughed sarcastically. "*A little!* Try one hundred and twelve at least."

"I had to get your attention somehow," Mom groaned, trying desperately to flip herself over.

"Well, you got it," the officer said, grinding her hand into my shoulder as she forced me down the porch steps. "My attention and a one-way trip straight to county jail."

No, no, no. This was all wrong. I hadn't had time to finish putting together the clues to figure out why Thompson would want to murder Harlow and then me. But I trusted my mom. If she said she saw him, then he was probably still here somewhere.

"Thompson!" I shouted, trying and failing to get away from my captor. "We know you're out there."

"Stop deflecting," the officer spat. Why wouldn't she just listen to us? If she hauled Mom and me away, then Nan would be in definite danger and Thompson would most likely never be brought to justice.

Officer Raines pushed me toward her cruiser with Nan hitting her every step of the way. "You let my granddaughter go!"

This was all going very wrong very fast. There was only one person left to turn to now. Well, not person exactly…

"Octo-Cat!" I screamed, craning my neck over my shoulder to glance back toward the house. "Help us!"

Right on cue, my dear, sweet tabby came running through his special electronic door flap and looked up at me with shaking eyes. "Angela, I'd never, ever hurt you."

"I know," I said tenderly, which was difficult considering I was still in police custody. "Help us. Help us catch Thompson. He's the killer, not the cats."

Officer Raines regarded me with a piteous look. *"You* might be able to get off on an insanity plea," she said, and clearly this dissatisfied her greatly.

Octo-Cat ran into the yard and started shouting at the top of his lungs. We all watched as he cried, "Jacques! Jillianne! Now is the time! Let us bring your human's killer to justice! Do as cats do! Do it now!"

I don't know whether he actually knew where they'd been hiding, but a moment later a terrible growl sounded on the roof, followed by a hiss, and...

Thompson staggered into view, away from the spot he'd been hiding in behind the turret. *My turret!*

"There he is!" I shouted to Officer Raines, twisting violently to force her to look.

"Sir," the cop shouted, spotting him at once. "Why are you trespassing here?"

"Oh, um," My boss sputtered, running hands over his suit jacket. His face had fresh blood dripping down the side, and I instantly recognized the work of one ticked-off kitty—maybe two.

Thompson reached beneath his jacket, then

pulled out a gleaming pistol. For the third time within a span of fifteen minutes, I was at risk of dying. What a day this was.

"Sir! Drop the weapon!" Officer Raines yelled, pushing me to the ground presumably for my safety.

Octo-Cat sprinted over to me and began to lick the dirt away from my cheek with his sandpaper tongue. "I'm so sorry, Angela. To think, I was used like that. I would never hurt you. You're my human, and I love you."

"I know," I said, wishing I wasn't cuffed so that I could stroke his soft, fluffy head. "I love you, too."

A terrible scream ripped us apart. I looked just in time to see Thompson hit the ground. His leg twisted at an unseemly angle following his two-story fall, and he cried out in tremendous pain.

Rolling onto my side, I looked up and saw the previously missing Jacques and Jillianne sitting at the edge of the roof licking their hairless paws happily. And suddenly it all clicked into place. I still didn't know why he'd done it, but Thompson had used the Sphynxes to trip the senator the same way he'd used Octo-Cat to trip me, the intelligent jerk. No wonder the poor, distraught cats had confessed to the crime.

Octo-Cat glanced toward Jacques and Jillianne on the roof and cried in delight. "They did as cats do!" he enthused, rushing toward Thompson's prostrate form.

What happened next wasn't pretty. He walked right onto Thompson's back and popped a squat. A wet spot quickly darkened the light suit jacket, and the unmistakable smell of ammonia mixed with the fresh evening air..

"That's for trying to kill my human!" he yelled, proceeding to scratch Thompson with his hind legs in a fury.

Nan laughed and clapped her hands together. Honestly, I'd have done the same if I wasn't cuffed at that particular moment. "Wonderful," she squealed.

"Officer Raines," I mumbled, my face squashed to the ground. "That man broke into my house and tried to kill me. We're pretty sure he's also the one who killed Senator Harlow and tried to make it look like an accident."

Thompson just moaned in agony.

"You're lucky a fall like that didn't snap your neck," the policewoman said, taking the cuffs off me and my mom, then going over to snap a pair on Thompson. "Or maybe not, seeing as you're going to have a lot of explaining to do once we get you to the station."

She forced him onto his feet, and he cried out in pain again.

"Serves you right!" Nan shouted as Officer Raines stuffed him in the back of her cruiser and fled into the night.

So, now that we knew whodunnit, it was time to figure out why…

CHAPTER NINETEEN

M om, Nan, and I gathered around the formal dining table, the same table that had been used to serve the poisonous meal that caused the late owner of this estate to lose her life. I tried not to think about that too much, though, as I dug into the delicious and hard-earned meal before me.

Despite our posh surroundings, we were eating tuna noodle casserole with a Vienna sausage and breadcrumb topping.

"I can't believe Mr. Thompson killed his friend. I can't believe he tried to kill *me*," I said, shaking my head sadly.

Octo-Cat sat beside me slurping a fresh dish of cream. He lifted his head, burped, and smiled at me unapologetically. It was amazing how quickly things reverted to normal around here.

"Well, you said he wasn't a very good boss," Nan pointed out, stabbing a mini sausage and taking a bite out of it, extreme bliss apparent on her face.

"Not a good boss and murderer seem miles apart to me," Mom pointed out. She'd found an old bottle of pinot noir in the cellar and was now taking generous sips from an overfull wine glass.

"You solved it," I said, giving her my best, most daughterly smile. "You're the one who figured everything out. *How?*"

She hesitated for a moment, took another drink, and then said, "Well, it wasn't easy, but I knew when the death had been ruled an accident that it just couldn't be the truth. Since you and Nan seemed to have formed your own investigative club, I decided to stake out the forest and watch. It's what any good journalist in my position would do."

"And then you saw Thompson creeping around," I provided.

"Yes. It was especially suspicious when I saw him climbing out of a second-story window. Invited guests just don't do that." She took another slow sip and sighed. "I still don't know why, though."

"Harlow was planning to retire. She was grooming him for her spot," I revealed. "Charles told me earlier today."

"Hey, you never told me that!" Nan protested, setting her fork down and pressing a napkin to her lips.

"I didn't tell either of you. I didn't get the chance."

"So, it seems," Mom said, rubbing her finger around the top of her wine glass as she spoke. "That Charles tipped off Thompson, which is why he came sneaking around here."

"Charles would never put me in danger," I argued, dread pooling in my stomach once again.

"Not knowingly," Nan agreed. "Do you think he was tricked?"

"It was my fault," I mumbled, seeing now what had happened. "I asked Charles to talk to him about why he'd visited the crime scene on day one."

"And that conversation was enough for him to know that you were on to him," Nan said with a scowl. "I never did much care for that man."

"You also never met him," I pointed out,

loving how ready and willing both my mom and my nan were to come to my defense.

"They were friends," Mom said after a few silent moments passed. "He killed a friend. For what, power?"

"I honestly don't know," I said. "Maybe Officers Raines and Bouchard will be able to get it out of him, though."

"I really hope we've seen the last murder in Glendale for many years to come," Nan added with a sigh.

"I don't," Mom said, raising her glass. When Nan and I both turned to her aghast, she said, "What? It makes for good news."

"I'm with her," Octo-Cat said from his spot beside me. "I've never had this much fun in all my lives."

We finished supper and mom went home. I realized too late that Cal hadn't gotten the chance to deliver Nan's bed, but she seemed nonplussed by this.

"I like sleeping in the window seat," she said. "It's like an adventure."

I rolled my eyes but headed to bed all the same.

Octo-Cat followed a few paces behind me. "Angela?" he asked. "Are we okay?"

We both got into my bed, and I stroked his back. "Of course we're okay. It wasn't your fault."

He hung his head and moved out of my reach. "I should have tried harder. I should have helped more with the Sphynxes."

"Yes, you should have," I agreed, unwilling to waver on this one specific truth. "But we can't change the past. Only try to do better tomorrow."

Octo-Cat purred and rolled onto his back. "You may pet my belly now," he informed me.

I hesitated with my fingers hanging about an inch from his furry underside. "Do you promise not to bite me?"

"I promise not to bite you ever again," he said. Well, that was an empty promise, if I'd ever heard one. No matter how euphoric and in love with me he felt now, tomorrow would come and I'd no doubt find myself on his bad side once more. I didn't doubt his intentions, though.

For tonight, I decided to relax a little and let myself enjoy his unexpected kindness. I petted him for a while longer, until my phone buzzed beside us.

"Just a sec," I said, shifting the call to speaker. "Hello?"

"It's Charles," my friend said, out of breath.

A huge smile stretched across my face. "I know."

"I'll leave you to your boyfriend," Octo-Cat announced, trotting out of my room and off into some other part of the house. I was happy Charles couldn't understand him, especially since he was still very much in a relationship with Breanne Calhoun and I still didn't know what would come of my new crush on her twin brother, Cal.

"I heard what happened with Thompson," he said. His voice cracked, and it sounded as if he might be crying. "The police came by to question me tonight. They thought since I was his partner, I might have been involved."

"They know you weren't, right?" I ground out, absolutely unwilling to let Charles take the fall for this. He was only involved in the first place because I asked for his help.

"It's my fault he came after you." His voice cracked again. "If anything had happened to you, Angie—"

"Stop. Nothing happened. I'm fine. What about you? Did the police clear you yet?"

"Not officially, but I'm sure it's just a matter of time."

"I'm still trying to figure out why Thompson would have killed his friend." I began chewing on my thumbnails again. Luckily, Charles couldn't see my disgusting habit and Mom wasn't here to swat me over it.

"I don't think he meant to," Charles answered. "My guess is he just wanted to hurt her enough to get her to step down early so he could take her place."

"But why?"

"Hopefully he'll confess whatever his motives were, but I'm willing to guess he and Harlow disagreed when it came to the proposed pipeline. They both loved the environment, but Thompson may have been more willing to bend his ethics for the right price."

"That's awful," I spat, then wiped my mouth with the back side of my arm.

"Yeah, it is," Charles agreed. "But you promise you're okay?"

"I promise," I assured him. "Hey, I hear congrats are in order. You bought Nan's house."

He laughed. "Oh, that. Yeah, I have fond memories of our time working the Calhoun case there together."

"Good night, Charles," I said with a huge smile on my face. Maybe I still had a chance with Charles after all.

"You done?" Octo-Cat asked, standing just outside the open door.

"Yeah. Do I get more cuddles now?" I asked, patting the bed beside me.

He glowered at me. "Angela, not in front of company!" He stepped aside to reveal Jacques and Jillianne who also stood waiting in the hall. They couldn't understand me like Octo-Cat could, but apparently that was beside the point.

"Sorry," I mumbled and sat up in bed. "C'mon in."

All three cats entered and found comfy spots on top of my comforter.

I waited for Octo-Cat to explain what was going on, and after a short awkward silence, he did. "I know you still have questions about what happened, so I went and found these two and brought them here for you."

"But you hate the Sphynxes," I whispered,

covering my mouth just in case they could somehow read my lips.

Octo-Cat shrugged. "They're annoying, but also kind of cool. Did you see the way they knocked that guy right off the roof? It was awesome."

I laughed and reached forward to touch the small Sphynx, Jacques. His bare skin was surprisingly soft—not slippery and cold like I expected.

Jillianne came forward to request pets, too, but Octo-Cat hopped onto my lap and meowed a warning. "Paws off my human!" he shouted.

I just laughed again. I loved when Octo-Cat took pride in our relationship. Since he had no problem insulting me freely, I knew his compliments also came straight from the heart.

"Okay," he said once they'd both retreated to the end of the bed. "What do you want to know?"

"You mentioned a red dot when you—I mean, when I fell. Did they see a red dot, too?"

The cats exchanged meows back and forth, and for once I just sat back and enjoyed the spectacle. A few minutes later, Octo-Cat had his report. "Yes, a shiny red dot. The laser pointer."

"If you know it's a laser pointer, then why do you chase it?" I asked him.

He turned toward the Sphynxes, but I interrupted. "No, I'm asking you that."

"It's not a decision we make to chase the shiny red dot," he told me gravely. "Some things just are. Like how the sun rises, the rooster crows, the cat also chases the shiny red dot."

"Who's talking in riddles now?" I asked with a smirk. "That was incredibly poetic."

He rolled his eyes. "Do you want me to help you or not?"

"Yes, please." I gave him an apologetic pat on the head. "Would you please ask why they always sat in that cold corner?"

"Oh, I already know that, too," Octo-Cat said. "They were punishing themselves."

"Punishing themselves?" I asked, feeling so sorry for those poor hairless kitties.

He nodded. "Cats love warmth, and these guys need it even more than the rest of us. They felt so bad about killing their human, they decided to punish themselves for it."

"Do they know it's not their fault?"

He shook his head. "I'm not sure. I tried explaining it to them, but they're still pretty upset."

"Aww, poor things," I cooed, shifting myself to the end of the bed so I could pet them again.

"Angela, we are not keeping them," Octo-Cat warned.

"That's okay," I said with a smile, giving him another soothing pet. "I already have the perfect cat, and besides, I think I already know the perfect person to take them in."

CHAPTER TWENTY

It's been a couple weeks since Nan, Octo-Cat, and I moved into our new home, and now it really does feel like home. The best part—well, other than us all being together, of course—is the new home library Cal made just for me. I moved my desk in there and now spend hours, reading, researching, or just browsing social media. I try to stay better informed about current events now that current events almost got me killed.

Mom couldn't be prouder.

My former boss, Mr. Thompson, pled guilty to manslaughter. As Charles had suspected, he never meant to kill the late senator Lou Harlow—just rough her up a bit. He confessed to tampering with the stairs and slipping something into her drink at the charity fundraiser that night. And, yes, he'd used her own cats against her. By means of a shiny red dot, Jacques and Jillianne ended up becoming a deadly murder weapon. Thompson had meant for the entire thing to look like an accident, but he hadn't counted on me and my team of super sleuths getting involved.

He claims he hadn't tried to kill *me*, either— only give me a fright—but I was not buying it. He didn't need to convince me, though. He didn't really need to convince anyone, because he'd already been disbarred and would never ever get the chance to serve in the Senate. Now it was merely a question of how much jail time he would get. I hoped it would be a lot.

Jacques and Jillianne finally seem to have forgiven themselves, and though they missed their former owner dearly, they now have a really good cat dad. It wasn't Matt who adopted them both, but rather Charles Longfellow, III. I knew he'd been lonely ever since Yo-Yo the Yorkie moved out and, seeing as he was putting down roots, two kitty roommates seemed the perfect way to make a house a home.

He didn't even find them creepy. I guess being

from California meant he could handle a lot of weird things without so much as batting an eye.

The senator's son, Matt, decided to stay in Blueberry Bay, too. He said he wanted to continue his mother's legacy and is currently battling his ex for summer custody of their two kids. He hopes to give them the kind of dreamy, ocean-side childhood he had growing up. He makes a nice neighbor now that I'm not afraid of him anymore, although he does plan on selling and moving into some place smaller so he has more money to contribute to the Lou Harlow Scholarship Fund.

The late senator left her mark on Washington, too. While Matt was sorting through her things, he found a mostly finished proposal for a new wind turbine farm, right here in the great state of Maine. She hadn't gotten the chance to present it to her Senate committee yet, but Matt is making sure it gets into the right hands.

So, everything's getting wrapped up nicely. Not exactly with a bow, but… you take what you can get.

Now we just had one major matter left to handle, and that would happen today. My new doorbell chimed, playing a cute old-timey jingle that Nan picked out from the huge list of options.

"Coming!" I cried racing down the stairs and flinging open the door.

Mom looked nervous, but I wasn't. I gave her a tight squeeze and then led her up to my new library.

She gasped at the big reveal. "Oh, Angie. It's a dream."

I motioned for her to take a seat at the window. I'd already opened it wide to let the balmy spring air circulate through the room. This room was no longer a prison, but rather a sanctuary.

"It is," I agreed with a blissful sigh. "But that's not why I invited you here today."

"Oh?" Mom folded her hands in her lap and waited.

"There's someone I want you to meet. *Octo-Cat!*" I hollered, and seconds later my kitty partner in crime came running to join us.

Mom laughed. "I already know Octo-Cat," she said, reaching out to stroke his soft, striped head.

I smiled and shook my head. "Not like I do. Do you want to talk to him?"

Her brows pinched together, and her eyes darted from me to Octo-Cat and back again. "How?"

"Through me." I put my hand on top of hers, and her eyes lit up with true mirth.

"Really?"

"Really." I squeezed her hands and let go.

Mom couldn't hide her excitement even if she'd tried. "I have so many questions! How does it work? Can you understand other animals, too? Can he understand me? How does the coffee maker factor into all of this?"

I laughed again. Mom's face fell, but I wrapped an arm around her to show her that it was okay.

"Those are all good questions," I said. "Let's take them one at a time."

WHAT'S NEXT?

Apparently I've been slacking on the job as a paralegal, even though the firm doesn't know that I'm secretly working as the area's premier Pet Whisperer P.I. to solve our toughest cases behind the scenes. Now they've hired an intern to "help" me manage my workload…

But what the partners don't realize is that they've let a nefarious criminal into our offices. Trust me—Octo-Cat can smell this guy's stink from a mile away.

The worst part? I'm pretty sure he can talk to animals, too… and he most definitely isn't using his talents to solve crimes and defend the innocent.

I've always wondered how that zap from an

old coffeemaker landed me with supernatural abilities. Now it's time to find out once and for all. Otherwise I fear I may wind up losing them—and my trusty talking feline sidekick—for good.

Pre-order to save! DOG-EARED DELINQUENT is just 99 cents until it releases on June 27.

SNEAK PEEK OF DOG-EARED DELINQUENT

Hi, I'm Angie Russo, and my life is way harder than you'd expect for someone who lives in an old East Coast mansion. Well, it's not really my house —more like my cat's. After all, it's his trust fund that pays the bills.

It may seem like I've won the lottery, but think again. Times are tricky when you have a talking cat bossing you around day in and day out.

Yeah, I said it.

My cat can talk.

As in, we communicate, have conversations, understand each other. I'm not sure how or why our strange connection works, only that it does. And as much as I wished I knew more, sometimes you just have to accept things at face value. It all happened so fast, too. I went to work unable to talk to animals, got zapped by a faulty coffee maker, got knocked unconscious, and when I woke up again—*bada bing, bada boom!*—now I'm talking kitty.

I've decided to think of it as a stroke of fate, because it really does feel like Octo-Cat and I were meant to find each other. In the past six months alone, we've worked together to solve three separate murder investigations. I guess that's why I'm considering my mom's advice and officially looking into starting a business. She's dubbed me Pet Whisperer P.I.—not because I want anyone else to know about my strange abilities, but because we needed some kind of excuse for me to take Octo-Cat around on my sleuthing calls.

After all, I wouldn't be much of a Sherlock without my Watson. Okay, *I'm* probably the Watson in our relationship. If you've ever been owned by a cat, then you should understand.

Regardless, I'll be the first to admit that my whole life changed for the better once Octo-Cat became a part of it. Before then, I was just drifting from one thing to the next. I'd already racked up seven associate degrees due to my unwillingness to commit to any one major long enough to secure a bachelor's.

I guess you could say nothing ever felt quite like the perfect fit, but I kept trying anyway. I knew that somewhere out there my dream job was waiting... even if I didn't quite know what it was yet.

You see, greatness kind of runs in my family, and for the longest time I'd worried that particular trait had skipped right past me without a second thought.

My nan had followed her dreams to become a Broadway star back in her glory days, and my mom was the most respected news anchor in all of Blueberry Bay. My dad lived his dream, too, by doing the sports report on the same channel that featured Mom.

Now at last, after so much yearning, so much searching, wishing, and praying, I've found the career path that fits me like a glove—and that's private investigating. So what if I'm not getting paid for it yet? I probably could if I threw everything I had at getting my P.I. business up and off the ground.

But I'm scared of letting down the good people of Longfellow, Peters, & Associates. Oh, that's right. My favorite frenemy Bethany is the newest partner, and I am so proud of her. Between her and Charles, I know the firm is in the best possible hands, but quitting to pursue self-employment?

That's downright terrifying.

True, I'm only part-time at the moment, but the twenty hours per week I put in are really well spent. I know I'm making a difference, and yet...

Aargh. I've never had this much trouble quitting a job before. Why can't I just hand in my two weeks' notice and say, "See ya around!?"

Maybe part of me still longs for the chance to see where Charles and I could take our relationship, provided he's willing to ditch his annoying realtor girlfriend. Or maybe I don't want to leave Bethany behind when we've worked so hard to overcome our differences.

It's also likely that I'm afraid of spending all day and all night at home with my crabby tabby for company. Nan lives with us now, too, but Octo-Cat reserves all his whining just for me. I mean, I guess it makes sense seeing as I'm the one who understands him.

At the end of the day, life sometimes requires hard decisions.

Historically, I'm not so great at making them.

If I just give it a few more weeks, maybe the right answer will fall into my lap. Yeah, I like that idea.

Until that happens, though, I'll just continue to wait and pray I get the courage to ask for what I really need. First, I'll have to make sure it's actually what I want, and then...

Watch out, world! I'm Angie Russo, and I'm coming for you.

"I come bearing muffins!" I cried as I bounded into the firm ten minutes late that morning. I still had a hard time calculating my new commute, but I hoped that Nan's homemade baked goods would more than make up for my tardiness.

"Ahem," somebody cleared his throat from the desk near the door. *My* desk.

I whipped around so fast, I fumbled my beautiful basket of muffins and dropped them straight onto the floor. All of Nan's hard work was ruined in an instant. It was a good thing she enjoyed baking so much and probably already had another fresh batch ready and waiting at home.

"Let me help you," the stranger said, rushing over to offer assistance I most definitely didn't need. I watched him from the corner of my eye, still refusing to acknowledge this interloper's presence. From what I could discern, he was tall and gangly, with white blond hair and thick, emo glasses.

"Oh, good," Bethany said, clasping her hands together as she strode toward us both with a smile. "You've met Peter."

"Peter?" I asked with a frown as the new guy stuck his hand out toward me in greeting. Looking at him straight on now, I saw he wore his dress shirt open with a t-shirt underneath that read *Awake? Yes. Ready to do things? Ha, ha, ha!* Charming.

The disturbing top half was paired with wrinkly cargo khakis on bottom. Fulton and Thompson *never* would have let this fly in their days. Yeah, I knew the firm was mostly better off without them, but, still couldn't we at least try to look like professionals here?

"You're Angie, right?" Peter asked, grabbing one of the muffins that hadn't touched the floor and shoving it into his mouth with wide eyes. "*Mmm,*" he said pointing at it. "So good."

I disliked this guy more and more by the

moment, but Bethany seemed so excited to intro-
duce us that I forced a smile and shook his hand
despite my better judgement.

"Peter's our new intern," she explained. "He's
going to help you manage your workload."

"I don't need help managing my workload," I
shot back, recoiling from Peter's grasp when he
wouldn't let my hand go after the normal, polite
period of time for a greeting.

Bethany frowned. "Not exactly true. It's been
harder for all of us since you switched to part-
time, but it's okay, because Peter is the perfect
person to step in and smooth things out."

Yeah, me going part-time was the problem
and not the revolving door of partners we'd seen
so far this year. "What exactly are his qualifica-
tions?" I asked, regarding him coldly.

Peter popped the remains of that precious
blueberry muffin into his mouth and mumbled,
"I'm her cousin, and I work for minimum
wage."

Bethany shot him a dirty look, finally showing
me that he bugged her, too. That at least made
me feel a little better about all this. "Really, Peter.
You need to stop being so liberal about sharing
your salary."

"Sorry," he muttered with a shrug that suggested he really couldn't care less about it.

Why was he here? I may not be the best paralegal in the world, but I was miles better than this guy. He probably didn't even have his degree. This was all wrong. I couldn't quite say why exactly, only that I hated everything about this Peter guy.

"Wait," I said, realizing something. "Your name is Peter Peters? You sound like a super hero."

"Or a super villain," he countered with another shrug and a strange new smile.

"Anyway," Bethany said, glancing at her feet to make sure no errant muffin crumbs had attached themselves to her shiny patent pumps. "This is Peter's first day, which is why I asked him to come in a bit early. Can you help get him set up? Show him the ropes?"

"What kind of ropes?" I demanded. I didn't normally start my work day by playing babysitter to some annoying nepotistic hire.

No, right now, I was supposed to be in Bethany's office while she safely brewed me a cup of delicious, life-saving coffee. There was no way I'd touch another coffee maker as long as I lived, but I still enjoyed the extra jolt it gave me when someone else was willing to brave the brew master.

"Just the stuff you normally do," Bethany answered with a dismissive gesture, already turning to take her leave. "If either of you need me, I'll be in my office. I have client meetings most of the morning, but should be free around lunch time."

"Okay, bye," I said, turning to my new charge, resigned that I would have pretty much the worst work half-day ever.

He smiled after his cousin. "Too-da-loo!" he called, waggling his fingers, then turned to me. "Okay, so I'm ready to learn how to be you when I grow up," he announced.

He did not just say that!

Well, so much for turning in my notice. There was no way I could leave the firm with this bumbling oaf of a paralegal. If only we could cue a makeover montage in real life. I'd choose one of my favorite upbeat 80's pop jams, spend a few minutes reforming him, then call it done and move on. Real life never worked fast enough.

"Let's go set up your email," I said with a sigh,

leading him back to my desk that we now seemed to be expected to share.

"Cool, cool. And when do I get my company-issued iPhone?" He bobbed his head, following after me like a lost little duckling.

"What? Why would we give you an iPhone?"

"Uh, hello. FaceTime." He twisted his hands and formed a rectangle about the size of a smart phone then looked at me through the gap.

And just like that, he went from simply irritating to downright terrifying. FaceTime was the same app I used to call my cat from work. Our senior partner, Charles, had found out when he was still brand new to the firm and bribed me to help him defend a client. Was it just a coincidence that this Peter Peters had alluded to it now?

Or did he know something that could get us both into very big trouble?

Oh, I did not like this. I did not like it one bit.

Pre-order to save! DOG-EARED DELINQUENT is just 99 cents until it releases on June 27.

WHAT'S AFTER THAT?

What's even worse than having a snarky talking tabby as your best friend?

When he inexplicably goes missing…

Octo-Cat is gone, and all the evidence suggests that he was taken on purpose. With the growing number of people the two of us have put behind bars, it's no surprise that someone's out for revenge.

But how will I ever manage to solve this particular crime without the help of my partner?

The only other person who might be able to help me just relocated to Georgia. But I'm desperate enough to try anything, including exposing my secret to the whole of Blueberry Bay. Anything to bring him home safe.

Oh, Octo-Cat. Where have you gone?

Pre-order to save! THE CAT CAPER is just $2.99 until it releases on July 31.

ABOUT MOLLY FITZ

While USA Today bestselling author Molly Fitz can't technically talk to animals, she and her doggie best friend, Sky Princess, have deep and very animated conversations as they navigate their days. Add to that, five more dogs, a snarky feline, comedian husband, and diva daughter, and you can pretty much imagine how life looks at the Casa de Fitz.

Molly lives in a house on a high hill in the Michigan woods and occasionally ventures out for good food, great coffee, or to meet new animal friends.

Writing her quirky, cozy animal mysteries is pretty much a dream come true, but sometimes she also sometimes goes by the name Melissa Storm (also a USA Today bestselling author, yay!) and writes a very different kind of story.

Learn more, grab the free app, or sign up for her newsletter at www.MollyMysteries.com!

MORE FROM MOLLY

If you're ready to dive right in to more Pet Whisperer P.I., then you can even order the next books right now. They are:

Kitty Confidential

Terrier Transgressions

Dog-Eared Delinquent

The Cat Caper

CONNECT WITH MOLLY

Sign up for Molly's newsletter for book updates and cat pics: **mollymysteries.com/subscribe**

Download Molly's app for cool bonus content: **mollymysteries.com/app**

Join Molly's reader group on Facebook to make new friends: **mollymysteries.com/group**

Made in the USA
Monee, IL
20 December 2020

55059348R00132